Silas placed a ⟨barcode: S0-ALK-675⟩ *arm*

"Please, don't go. I'm awful sorry for makin' ya mad."

She swallowed hard, struggling to keep her tears at bay. Silas was looking at her with those big brown eyes, and he really did look sorry. "I'm not exactly mad," she admitted. "I just get tired of everyone thinkin' I'm still a *kinder*." Her arms made a wide arc as she motioned toward the lake. "Could a child catch as many fish as I did today?" Before Silas had a chance to answer, she rushed on. "Could a little girl have fixed such a tasty picnic lunch or baked a batch of cookies you couldn't eat enough of?"

Silas studied her a few seconds, then in an unexpected gesture, he pulled her to his chest. "No, Rachel, only a feisty young woman coulda done all those things."

Rachel held her breath as he moved his fingers in gentle, soothing circles across her back. Was Silas about to kiss her? She wrapped her arms around his neck and nestled her head against his shoulder.

Then, as quickly as he'd embraced her, Silas pulled away. "Now that we've got that cleared up, how's about I get my binoculars and bird identification book, and the two of us can spend the next hour or so lookin' for some unusual feathered creatures?"

Rachel nodded as a sense of embarrassment rattled through her. Silas's sudden shift in mood hit her like a blow to the stomach and she cringed, wondering what he must have thought about her brazen actions. Even though it was Silas who initiated the hug, she had taken it one step further. Truth be told, Silas had never led her to believe he had any romantic feelings for her. The embrace was probably just a friendly, brotherly gesture.

WANDA E. BRUNSTETTER lives in Central Washington with her husband, who is a pastor. She has two grown children and six grandchildren. Her hobbies include doll repairing, sewing, ventriloquism, stamping, reading, and gardening. Wanda and her husband have a puppet ministry, which they often share at other churches, Bible camps, and Bible schools. Wanda invites you to visit her website: http://hometown.aol.com/rlbweb/index.html.

Books by Wanda E. Brunstetter

HEARTSONG PRESENTS
HP254—A Merry Heart
HP421—Looking for a Miracle
HP465—Talking for Two
HP478—Plain and Fancy

The Hope Chest

Wanda E. Brunstetter

Heartsong Presents

To my mother, Thelma Cumby. Thanks for giving me your special hope chest, so I could pass it down to my daughter, Lorine, who will someday give it to one of her girls.

A note from the author:
I love to hear from my readers! You may correspond with me by writing:

Wanda E. Brunstetter
Author Relations
PO Box 719
Uhrichsville, OH 44683

ISBN 1-58660-538-0

THE HOPE CHEST

All Scripture quotations are taken from the King James Version of the Bible.

All of the characters and events in this book are fictitious. Any resemblance to actual persons, living or dead, or to actual events is purely coincidental.

Cover design by Randy Hamblin.

PRINTED IN THE U.S.A.

one

Rat-a-tat-tat! Rat-a-tat-tat! Rachel Beachy would have recognized that distinctive sound anywhere. She tipped her head back, shielded her eyes from the glare of the late afternoon sun, and gazed up at the giant birch tree. Sure enough, there it was—a downy woodpecker. Its tiny claws were anchored to the trunk of the tree, its petite head bobbing rhythmically in and out.

Hoping for a better look, Rachel decided to climb the tree. As she threw her leg over the first branch, she was glad she was alone and no one could see how ridiculous she looked. She'd never really minded wearing long dresses. After all, that was what Amish girls and women were expected to wear. However, there were times, such as now, when Rachel wished she could wear a pair of men's trousers. It certainly would make climbing trees a might easier.

Rachel winced as a piece of bark scratched her knee, leaving a stain of blood that quickly seeped through her dress. To Rachel, it was worth the pain if it would allow her to get a better look at that cute little wood-tapper.

Pik-pik! The woodpecker's unusual call resonated against the trunk. *Rat-a-tat-tat!*

"Such a busy little bird," Rachel said softly as it came into view, just two branches above where she sat straddling the good-sized limb. *Sure do wish I had my notebook along so's I could write down a few things about this beautiful creature the Lord made. God knows every bird in the mountains and the creatures of the field. It says so in Psalm 50.*

Rachel was about to move up one more limb, but a deep male voice drew her attention to the ground. "Hey, Anna, slow down once, would ya?"

Rachel dropped so her stomach was flat against the branch. She lifted her head slightly and peeked through the leaves. Her older sister sprinted across the open field, and Silas Swartley was a few feet behind. He ran like a jackrabbit, with his hands cupped around his mouth, yelling to beat the band. "Anna! Wait up!"

Rachel knew she'd be in big trouble if Anna caught her spying, so she held real still and prayed the couple would soon move on.

Anna stopped near the foot of the tree and Silas quickly joined her. "I wanna talk to ya, Anna," he panted.

Rachel's heart slammed into her chest. *Why couldn't it be me Silas wants to talk to? If only he could see that I'd be much better for him. If he knew how much I cared, would it make a difference?* Rachel knew Silas only had eyes for Anna. He'd been in love with her since they were *kinder,* and Rachel had loved Silas nearly that long as well. He was all the things she wanted in a man—good-looking, kindhearted, interested in birds, and he enjoyed fishing. . . .

She was sure he had many other attributes that made him so appealing, but with Silas standing right below her tree, she could barely breathe, much less think of all the reasons she loved him so much.

Rachel looked down at her sister, arms folded across her chest, standing there like a wooden statue. It was almost as if she couldn't be bothered with talking to Silas. It made no sense, for Anna and Silas had been friends a long time, and Silas had been coming over to their place to visit ever since Rachel could remember.

Silas reached for Anna's hand, but she jerked it away. "Just who do ya think you are, Silas Swartley?"

"I'm your boyfriend, that's who. Have been since we were *kinder,* and you know it."

"I don't know any such thing, so don't go tryin' to put words in my mouth."

Rachel stifled a giggle. *That sister of mine. . .she's sure got herself a temper.*

Silas tipped his head to one side. "I don't get it. One minute you're sweet as cherry pie and the next minute ya act as if ya don't care for me a'tall."

Rachel knew Silas was speaking the truth. She'd seen with her own eyes the way Anna led that poor fellow on. Why, just last week she'd let him bring her home from a singing. There had to be some kind of interest on her part if she was willing to accept a ride in his courting buggy.

Rachel held her breath as Silas reached out to touch the ties on Anna's *Kapp.* Anna jerked her head real quick, causing one of the ribbons to tear loose. "Now look what you've done!" Anna jerked the covering off her head and stuffed it inside the pocket of her black apron.

Silas removed his broad-brimmed straw hat, revealing a crop of dark, Dutch-bobbed hair. He planted the hat on top of Anna's head. "Here, you can wear my hat now."

Anna yanked it right off, but in so doing, the pins holding her hair in a bun must have been knocked loose, for a cascade of soft, tawny brown fell loosely down her back.

Rachel wished she could see the look on Silas's face. She could only imagine what he must be thinking as he reached up to scratch the back of his head. "I know Amish women aren't supposed to wear their hair down in public, but I sure wish you could, Anna." He groaned softly. "Why, you're prettier than a field full of fireflies at sunset!"

Rachel nearly gagged. It was sickening the way Silas got

so sappy over Anna. Especially when she didn't seem to appreciate all his attentions.

Anna rocked from side to side, kind of nervous-like. "Sometimes I wish I could cut my hair short, the way many English women do. Long hair can be such a bother, and anyways, it serves no real purpose."

"It does when ya wear it like that," Silas murmured.

Rachel gulped. *What I wouldn't give to hear Silas talk to me thataway. Maybe if I keep on hopin'. Maybe if. . .*

Rachel's thoughts took her to the verse she'd read in the book of Psalms that morning. *"But I will hope continually, and will yet praise thee more and more."*

Rachel would gladly offer praises to God if she could only win Silas's heart. Truth be told, the verse she should call her own might best be found in the book of Job. "My days are swifter than a weaver's shuttle and are spent without hope." She'd most likely end up an old maid, while Anna would have a *wunderbaar* husband and a whole house full of *kinder.*

"It don't make much sense to have long hair when you have to wear it pinned up all the time," Anna said, handing the straw hat back to Silas and pulling Rachel out of her musings.

"Are you questionin' the Amish ways, young lady?" Silas scolded playfully. "Now, what would your *mamm* and *daed* have to say about that?" Before Anna could answer, he added, "You've always been a bit of a rebel, haven't ya, now?"

Anna leaned against the tree, and Rachel dug her fingernails into the bark of the branch she was lying on. *What will my sister say to that comment?*

"I know there's some things about the Amish ways that are *gut,* but I feel so restricted," Anna said with a deep sigh.

Silas knelt on the grass beneath Anna's feet. "Can ya give me an example of what you're talkin' about?"

Rat-a-tat-tat! Rat-a-tat-tat! Pik! Pik!

"Say, that sounds like a woodpecker to me," Silas said, leaning his head back and looking up into the birch tree where Rachel was hiding.

She froze in place. If Silas should spot her instead of the bird, she'd be caught like a piggy trying to get into Mom's flower garden. Anna would sure as anything think she'd climbed the tree just to spy on her and Silas.

"Forget about the dumb old woodpecker," Anna said impatiently. "I'm trying to tell you why I don't like bein' Amish no more."

Silas stood up and peered into the branches. "Hmm. . .I know I heard him, but I sure don't see that old rascal anywhere."

"You and your dopey bird-watchin'! One would think you've never seen a woodpecker before." Anna moaned. "Rachel's fascinated with birds, too. Why, I believe she'd rather be watchin' them eat from one of our feeders than eatin' a meal herself."

Silas looked away from the tree and turned to face Anna. "Birds are interestin' little creatures, but you're right. . .I can do my bird-watchin' some other time." He touched her shoulder. "Now what were ya gonna say about bein' Amish?"

"Take these clothes, for example," Anna announced. "Women shouldn't have to wear long dresses all the time. They only get in the way."

Rachel sucked in her breath. Where was this conversation headed? If Anna wasn't careful, she'd be saying something plumb stupid and maybe even getting into all kinds of trouble for shooting off her big mouth. Especially if the bishop got wind of it. Anna had been acting a bit strange here of late—disappearing for hours at a time and saying some mighty peculiar things. Her conversation with Silas was only confirming what Rachel already suspected. Anna was dissatisfied with the Amish way of life. It wasn't like Anna climbed trees and saw her dress as a hazard. No, Rachel's prim and proper sister wouldn't be caught dead up in a tree. Rachel knew there was a lot more that bothered Anna about being Amish than wearing long dresses. She'd heard her complain about other things as well.

"What would you suggest women wear—trousers?" Silas asked, jerking Rachel's attention back to the conversation below.

"I think it's only fair that women and girls should have the freedom of wearin' long pants if they want to," Anna replied stiffly.

"Are ya sayin' you'd wear men's trousers if ya could?"

"Maybe I would, and maybe I wouldn't. I sure could do my chores much easier if I didn't have a long skirt gettin' in the way all the time." Anna paused, and Rachel shifted her legs, trying to get a bit more comfortable. "Maybe I'd be a whole lot happier if I'd been born English."

Oh, great! Now you've gone and done it, Rachel fumed. *Why can't ya just be nice to Silas instead of tryin' to goad him into an argument? Can't ya see how much the fellow cares for you? If anyone should be wantin' to wear men's trousers, it's me—Rachel, the tomboy. At least I've got the sense not to announce such a thing. And sayin' you should have been born English is just plain stupid.*

"I, for one, am mighty glad you're not English!" Silas said, his voice rising an octave.

"Humph! If I weren't Amish, I could wear whatever I please whenever I wished to do so."

"Listen here, Anna," he argued, "you shouldn't even be thinkin' such thoughts, much less speaking 'em. Why, if your *daed* ever heard ya say anything like that, you'd be in big trouble, and that's for certain sure!"

Anna moved away from the tree. "Let's not talk about this anymore. I need to be gettin' home. Rachel was way ahead of me when we left the river, so she's probably already there and has done half my chores by now. Mom let me have the afternoon off from workin' in the greenhouse, so I don't want her gettin' after me for shirking my household duties."

Rachel watched as Silas plopped the straw hat back on his head. "Yeah, well, I guess I need to be headin' for home, too." He made no move to leave and she had to wonder what was up.

Anna rolled and pinned her hair into place. Then she reached inside her pocket and retrieved the head covering, securing it back in place. She started walking away, but Silas stepped right up beside her. "I still haven't said what I wanted to say."

"What'd ya wanna say?"

Silas shuffled his feet a few times, gave his suspenders a good yank, then cleared his throat real loud. "I. . .uh. . .was wonderin' if I might come a-callin' one evenin' next week."

Rachel's heart skipped a beat and she focused real hard on getting it to work right again. Silas had been sweet on Anna a good many years, so she should have known the day would come when he'd ask to start courting her. Only trouble was, if Anna started courting Silas, Rachel's chances would be nil. Oh, she just couldn't bear to think about it!

"Callin'? You mean, call on *me?*" Anna asked in obvious disbelief.

"Of course, Silly. Who'd ya think I meant—your little sister, Rachel?"

That's what I wish you meant. Rachel's pulse quickened at the thought of her being Silas's girlfriend. She drew in a deep breath and pressed against the tree limb as though she were hugging it. No sense hoping and dreaming the impossible. She knew Silas didn't care about her in the least. Not in the way he did Anna, that's for sure. To him, Rachel was just a girl, five years younger than he at that.

"We've known each other for many years, and ya did take

a ride in my courtin' buggy," Silas continued. "Now I think it's high time—"

"Hold on to your horses," Anna cut in. "You're a nice man, Silas Swartley, and a *gut* friend, but I can't start courtin' you."

Rachel could only imagine how Silas was feeling about now. Her tender heart went out to him. She wondered how her sister could be so blind. Couldn't Anna see how *wunderbaar* Silas was? Didn't she realize what a *gut* husband he would make? *At least for me,* Rachel lamented.

"I'm sorry if I've hurt your feelin's." Anna spoke so softly that Rachel had to strain to hear the words. "It's just that I have lots of dreams, and—"

"There's no need to explain," Silas said, cutting her off in midsentence. "You may think I'm just a big dumb Amish boy, but I'm not as stupid as I might look, Anna Beachy."

"I never meant to say you were stupid. I just want ya to understand that it won't work for the two of us." There was a long pause. "Maybe my little sister *would* be better for you."

Yes, yes, I would! Rachel's heart pounded with sudden hope. She held her breath, waiting to hear what Silas would say next, but disappointment flooded her soul when he turned on his heels and started walking away.

"I'll leave ya alone for now, but when you're ready, I'll be waitin'," he called over his shoulder. *"Wann du mich mohl brauchst, dan komm Ich*—when you need me, I will come." He broke into a run and was soon out of sight.

Rachel released her breath and flexed her body against the unyielding limb. Hot tears pushed against her eyelids, and she blinked several times to force them back. At least Silas and Anna hadn't known she was here, eavesdropping on their private conversation. That would have ruined any chance she might ever have of catching Silas's attention. Not that she had any, really. Besides their age difference, Rachel was sure she wasn't pretty enough for Silas. She had pale blue eyes and straw-colored hair. Nothing beautiful about her. Anna, on the other hand, had been blessed with sparkling green eyes and hair the color of ripe peaches. Rachel was certain Anna would always be Silas's first choice, because she was *schnuck*. *Too bad I'm not cute. I wish I hadn't been born so plain.*

❧

When Rachel arrived home several minutes behind her sister, she found her brother Joseph working on an old plow out in the yard. A lock of sandy brown hair lay across his sweaty forehead, and his straw hat was lying on a nearby stump.

He looked up and frowned. "You're late! Anna's already inside, no doubt helpin' Mom with supper. You'd better get in there quick-like, or they'll both be pretty miffed."

"I'm goin'," Rachel said with a shrug. "And don't you be thinkin' you can boss me around." She scrunched up her nose. "You may be twenty-one and three years older than me, but you're not my keeper, Joseph Beachy."

"Don't go gettin' your feathers ruffled. You're crankier than the old red rooster when his hens are fightin' for the best pieces of corn." Joseph's forehead wrinkled as he squinted his blue eyes. "Say, isn't that blood I see on your dress? What happened? Did ya fall in the river and skin your knee on a rock?"

Rachel shook her head. "I skinned my knee, but it wasn't on a rock."

Joseph gave her a knowing look. "Don't tell me it was another one of your tree-climbin' escapades."

She waved a hand and started for the house. "Okay, I won't tell ya that."

"Let Mom know I'll be in for supper as soon as I finish with the plow," he called after her.

As Rachel stepped onto the back porch, she thought about all the chores she had to do. It was probably a good thing. At least when her hands were kept busy, it didn't give her nearly so much time to think about things—especially Silas Swartley.

❧

Silas kicked a clump of grass with the toe of his boot. What had come over Anna Beachy all of a sudden? How come she was friendly one minute and downright rude the next? Worse than that, when had she developed such a dissatisfaction with being Amish? Had it been there all along, and he'd been too blind to notice? Was Anna just going through some kind of a phase, like many *younga* did when they sowed their wild oats?

Silas clenched his fists and kept trudging toward home. *Lord, I love Anna, but is she really the woman for me? I could never hold to foolish notions 'bout women wearin' men's pants or cuttin' their hair off, and she knows it. I care for Anna, but she's sure mixed up in her thinkin'. Why, she even suggested I start courtin' her little sister.* He shook his head and muttered, "Is that woman simpleminded? Rachel's just a *kinder,* for goodness' sake. Guess I'd best be prayin' about all this, for Anna surely does need some help."

As Silas rounded the bend, his farm came into view. A closed-in buggy sat out front in the driveway, and he recognized the horse. It belonged to Bishop Weaver.

"Hmm. . .wonder what's up?" He shrugged. "Maybe Mom invited the bishop and his family for supper tonight."

Silas entered the kitchen a few minutes later and found his folks and Bishop Weaver sitting at the kitchen table, drinking tall glasses of lemonade.

"How's things?" Silas asked. "Is supper ready? I'm starved!"

Mom gave him a stern look over the top of her metal-framed reading glasses, which were perched on the middle of her nose. "Where's your manners, Son? Can't you say hello to our guest before ya start frettin' over food?"

Silas was none too happy about his mother embarrassing

him that way, but he knew better than to sass her back. Mom might be only half his size, but she could still pack a good wallop to any of her boys' backsides, and she didn't care how old they were!

"Sorry," Silas apologized as he smiled and nodded at the bishop. "When I saw your buggy, I thought maybe you had the whole family along."

Bishop Weaver shook his head. "Nope. Just me."

"The bishop came by to have a little talk with you," Pap said, running a hand through his slightly graying hair, then motioning Silas to take a seat.

"Me? What about?"

"Your friend, Reuben Yutzy," Bishop Weaver answered with a curt nod.

Silas took off his straw hat and hung it on a wall peg near the back door, then took a seat at the table. "What about Reuben?"

Bishop Weaver leaned forward and leveled Silas with a piercing gaze. "As you already know, Reuben works for a fancy English paint contractor in Lancaster."

Silas merely nodded in response.

"I hear tell Reuben's been seen with some worldly folks."

"As you just said, he works for the English."

"I'm talkin' about Reuben's off hours," the bishop said, giving his long, gray beard a few good yanks. "Word has it that he's been goin' to some picture shows and hangin' around with a group of English *younga* who like to party and get all liquored up."

Silas frowned deeply. "I see."

"You know anything 'bout this, Son?" Pap spoke up.

"No, why would I?"

"Reuben and you have been *gut* friends since you was *kinder*," Mom reminded.

Silas shrugged. "That's true, but he don't tell me everything he does."

"So, you're sayin' you don't know nothin' about Reuben bein' involved in the things of the world?" Bishop Weaver questioned.

"Not a thing." Silas scooted his chair back and stood up. "Now, if you'll excuse me, I'd best see to my chores before supper."

Outside, on the back porch, Silas drew in a deep, cleansing breath. What in the world was going on here? First Anna acting *Ab im Kopp*—off in the head—and now all these questions about Reuben? It was enough to make him downright nervous!

two

Mom was sitting in her wheelchair at the table, tearing lettuce into a bowl. "You're late, Rachel." She wiped her hands on a paper towel and reached for a tomato. "Anna said you left the river way before she did. What kept ya, Daughter?"

"I'm really sorry," Rachel said sincerely. "I did a little birdwatchin' on the way home, and Anna must have missed me somehow." *Of course she missed you. You were up in a tree,* a little voice reminded. Pushing the thought aside, Rachel went to the kitchen sink and pumped enough water to fill the pitcher she'd just plucked off the counter.

"It seems you and Anna have both been livin' in a dream world lately. Is this what summer does to my girls?"

"I can't help it if I enjoy studyin' God's feathered creatures," Rachel replied.

Anna turned from her job at the stove. "Sure is funny I never saw you on the way home. If you were lookin' at birds, then where exactly were you—up in a tree?"

Rachel felt her face flame. Up in a tree was exactly where she'd been, but she sure didn't want Anna to know that. She glanced down at the bloodstain on her dress, hoping it would go unnoticed. "It don't matter where I was," she said defensively. "The point is—"

"I know, I know. . .you were lookin' at some stupid bird." Anna snickered. "Silas is such a *kischblich* man. He likes watchin' birds, too, but I think it's a big waste of time."

Rachel bristled at her sister's insensitivity. Who did she think she was, calling Silas a silly man? Just because Anna didn't appreciate birds didn't mean Rachel or Silas shouldn't.

Truth of the matter, Anna didn't appreciate anything about Silas. In fact, she deserved to be reminded of how *wunderbaar* he was.

"Have ya heard anything from Silas Swartley lately?" Rachel asked. *See how Anna likes that topic of conversation.* "I happen to know he brought you home from a singin' awhile back. Seems to me he might wanna start courtin' pretty soon."

Mom's pale eyebrows lifted in obvious surprise. "Is that so, Anna? Might could be that you'll soon be makin' a weddin' quilt for your hope chest." She smiled sweetly. "Or would ya prefer I make one?"

Anna started stirring the pot of savory stew like there was no tomorrow. "It was just one ride in his buggy. Nothin' to get all excited about, so there's no need for either one of us to begin a weddin' quilt."

"Why not be excited?" Mom asked. "Silas has been hangin' around our place for years now, and your *daed* and I both think he's a right nice fellow. Besides, you're twenty-three years old already. Don'tcha think it's time ya begin thinkin' about marriage?"

Anna moved away from the stove and opened the refrigerator door. She withdrew a bunch of celery and took it over to the sink. "I'm thinkin' the stew needs a bit more of this," she said, conveniently changing the subject.

Rachel had begun setting the table, but she couldn't let the matter drop. "Silas is really sweet on Anna," she commented, giving her older sister a sidelong glance.

"Is that so?" Mom said, shifting her wheelchair to one side, making it easier for Rachel to reach around her. "A lovely quilt would sure as anything make a fine addition to someone's hope chest." She stared off into space, like she might be thinking about her own hope chest and the days when she'd been preparing for marriage.

"I'm really sorry if Silas thinks he's sweet on me," Anna said with a frown. "I just can't commit to someone I'm not in love with."

Mom clicked her tongue. *"Ach,* I didn't mean to interfere. Guess I jumped to the wrong conclusion, but seein' as how you and Silas have been friends for so long, and since ya let him bring ya home from a singin', I thought things were gettin' kinda serious."

"Anna has other things she wants to do with her life. I heard her say so," Rachel blurted out. The sudden realization of what she'd just said hit her full in the face and her hand went straight to her mouth.

"When did ya hear me say such things?" Anna asked, turning to face Rachel and leveling her with a look of concern.

Rachel shrugged and kept placing the silverware on the table. "I'm sure you said it sometime."

"What other things are ya wantin' to do with your life?" Mom asked, pushing the salad bowl to the center of the table.

Anna merely shrugged in response.

"If I had someone as *wunderbaar* as Silas Swartley after me, I'd sure marry him in an instant," Rachel asserted. Her face felt suddenly warm, and she scurried across the room, hoping nobody had noticed the blush that was surely staining her cheeks.

"My, my," Anna said with a small laugh. "If I didn't know better, I'd be thinkin' my little sister was in love with Silas."

"Rachel's only eighteen—too young for such thoughts!" Mom declared.

"How old were you when you fell in love with Dad?" asked Anna.

"Guess I wasn't much more'n nineteen," Mom admitted. "Still—"

The back door flew open, interrupting Mom's sentence. Twelve-year-old Elizabeth burst into the kitchen. Her long brown braids, which were supposed to be pinned at the back of her head, were hanging down her back and had come partially unbraided. "Perry won't let me have a turn on the swing. He's been mean to me all day!"

Mom shook her head. "You know your twin brother likes to tease. *Der gleh Deihenge*—the little scoundrel. I wish you would try to ignore it."

"But, Mom, Perry—"

Mom held up one hand to silence Elizabeth. "Run outside and call Dad and your brothers in for supper."

A short time later, the family was gathered around the huge wooden table. Dad sat at the head, with Joseph beside him, and Perry in the next seat. Mom was at the other end of the table, and Rachel, Anna, and Elizabeth sat directly across from the boys.

"Did ya get that old plow fixed today, Joseph?" Dad asked as he filled his plate with a generous helping of stew.

Joseph shrugged. "I can't be sure 'til I try it out in the fields, but I think it's probably workable again."

Dad pulled thoughtfully on his long brown beard, lightly peppered with gray. "No matter what those English neighbors of mine may think, I say ya just can't replace a reliable horse and plow!"

"Horses can be unreliable, too," Anna put in. "In fact, I've known 'em to be downright stubborn at times."

Dad gave her a curious look, but he made no comment.

"I've been wonderin'. . .don'tcha think we need to modernize a bit?" Anna asked. "I mean, workin' the greenhouse would go much better if we had electricity and a telephone. . . even one outdoors on a pole."

"We're Old Order Amish, Anna. Don't ever forget that," Dad reminded. "God's Word commands us to be separate. Although some in our community make a few concessions, I don't choose to live as the English do, and I never shall!"

Everyone was silent, but Rachel knew her sister well. She could sense the frustration Anna was feeling and wondered if she should say something on her behalf—before Anna spoke again and got herself into trouble. Rachel drew in a deep breath. What could she really say, though? She sure didn't agree with Anna's worldly thinking. In fact, Rachel loved everything about being Amish—especially one Amish man in particular.

Anna folded her arms across her chest in a stubborn, un-yielding pose, and a contrite look crossed her face. "I'd like to be excused."

Dad nodded, but Mom protested. "You've hardly eaten a thing."

"I'm not hungry." She lowered her head, causing her long lashes to form crescents against her pale cheeks.

Rachel looked down at her own plate. How could anyone not be hungry with a helping of Mom's delicious savory stew sitting before them?

"Let her go," Dad said. "Just might could be that goin' without supper is what she needs to help clear her head for better thinkin'."

Anna jumped up, nearly knocking over her glass of lemonade, and she stormed out of the room.

Rachel moved back against her chair, her shoulder blades making contact with the hard wood. *Such a silly one, my sister is. She just don't know how good she's got it, and that's for certain sure.*

❧

After supper, Rachel helped her mother and Elizabeth wash and dry the dishes, then clean up the kitchen. "Many hands make light work," Mom always said. Too bad Anna was upstairs sulking in her room. If she'd been helping, they probably could have been done already.

When the last dish was finally put away, Rachel turned to

her mother. "I think I'll go up and see how Anna's doin'. Unless you've got somethin' more for me here."

Mom shook her head. "Nothin' right now. In fact, I was just thinkin' about goin' outside to check on my garden." She glanced up at Elizabeth, who was drying her hands on a terry cloth towel. "How'd ya like to join your old *mamm* outside?"

Elizabeth wrinkled her freckled nose. "You ain't old."

Rachel glanced over at her mother. She was smiling from ear to ear; that sweet smile which made her so special. Even with her disability, Mom never complained. From all Rachel had been told, their mother had been confined to a wheel-chair most of her life. The story was that when Mom was a *kinder,* a tree branch fell during a bad storm. It hit her across the back and neck, and part of her spinal cord was damaged. Ever since then, Mom had either been in a wheelchair or strapped to a pair of crutches that made her walk all stiff-legged, like a wooden doll. However, she didn't let her disability hold her back much. In fact, Mom had been right independent when she was a *younga* and had first opened the greenhouse she'd named Grandma's Place.

Rachel smiled to herself as she thought of the stories Dad and Mom often told about their courting days and how they almost didn't marry. Mom had been convinced Dad only wanted her because he loved flowers so much and hoped to get his hands on her business. It took some doing, but Dad finally made her believe it was her he loved most. They got married, ran the greenhouse together, and a year later, little Anna was born. Mom thought it was a true miracle, the way God had allowed her to give birth. Rachel could only imag-ine how her mother must have felt when she kept having one miracle after another. First Anna, then two years later Joseph was born. Another three years went by, and Rachel came onto the scene. Mom must have thought she was done having *kinder,* because it was another six years before the twins made their surprise appearance.

Wow! Five miracles in all, Rachel mused. *I'll surely feel blessed if God ever gives me five children.* She drew in a deep breath and released it with such force that Mom gave her a strange look.

"You okay, Rachel? Ya looked kinda like you were day-dreamin' again."

Daydreaming was nothing new for Rachel. As far back as she could remember, she'd enjoyed fantasizing about things.

"I'm fine, Mom," she said with a nod. "Guess I *was* doin' a bit of dreamin', all right."

"Say, how'd ya get that blood on your dress?" Mom asked suddenly.

"Oh, just scraped my knee," Rachel replied with a shrug.

"Want me to take a look-see?"

"No, it's nothin'." Rachel smiled. "I'm ready to go up and see Anna now."

"Jah, you go ahead," Mom said. "Maybe you can talk some sense into her about courtin' Silas."

Upstairs, Rachel found Anna lying on her bed, staring at the plaster ceiling. "Mind if I join ya?"

"Why's Dad so stubborn?" Anna asked, not even bothering to answer Rachel's question. "Can't he see there's a place for some modern things? He's the reason I get so upset, ya know." A stream of tears ran down her cheeks, and she swiped at them with the back of her hand.

Rachel took a seat near the foot of Anna's bed. "People often blame things on the previous generation 'cause there's only one other choice."

Anna sat up, swinging her legs over the side of the bed. "What's that supposed to mean?"

"The other choice would be to put the blame on yourself."

Anna sucked in her protruding lip and blinked several times. "How dare you speak to me thataway! I can do whatever I like, and Dad can't make me do otherwise!" With one quick motion, she jerked off her head covering, and her golden brown locks came tumbling down the back of her dark green dress.

Rachel couldn't help but think of the things Silas had said when Anna's hair had been down earlier that day. It made her feel almost ill to realize Silas was in love with such a spiteful, rebellious woman.

Anna paced the room with quick, nervous steps. Suddenly she pointed to a pair of scissors, lying next to the sewing basket on her dresser. "Maybe I should cut my hair short." She leaned over, and her fingers were just inches from the scissors when Rachel's gasp stopped her.

"What do ya think you're doin'?" Rachel shouted. "Amish women don't have short hair and you know it!"

Anna pulled her hand slowly away. "If I weren't Amish, then I could do whatever I wanted with my hair, and my clothes, and—"

"But you are Amish, and you should be happy bein' such."

"Why? Why must I be happy bein' Amish?" Anna squinted her green eyes at Rachel. "Didn't God give each of us a mind of our own? Shouldn't I have the right to choose how I wanna live?"

Rachel nodded. "Of course you should, but you're already baptized into the church, and if you were to go against the *Ordnung* now, you'd be shunned, and that's a fact!"

Anna sniffed. "Don'tcha think I know that, Rachel? I feel like an impostor sometimes. I've thought long and hard on all of this, too."

"Then I hope you've come to the right conclusion. You've gotta learn to be happy with the Amish faith."

❧

Silas shielded his eyes from the glare of the morning sun as he strolled through the small town of Paradise. He'd come in early today with the intent of speaking to his friend, Reuben, who was painting on a new grocery store in town.

He found Reuben around the back of Larsen's Supermarket, holding a paintbrush in one hand and a giant oatmeal cookie in the other.

"I see you're hard at work," Silas said with a grin.

Reuben chuckled. "I do need to keep up my strength."

"*Jah,* I'm sure."

"What brings you to town so early?" Reuben asked as he applied a glob of paint to the side of the wooden building.

"I came to see you."

"So, now ya see me. What do ya think?"

Silas shook his head. "You're such a strange one. Always kiddin' around."

Reuben's blue eyes fairly sparkled, and he ran a hand through his blond hair, which was growing much too long for any self-respecting Amish man. Silas had to wonder how come his friend wasn't wearing his straw hat, either, especially on a day when the sun was already hot as fire. He was about to voice that question when Reuben asked a question of his own.

"You heard any good jokes lately?"

Silas shook his head. "Nope. You?"

Reuben nodded but kept right on painting. "My boss, Ed, told me a real funny one the other day, but I don't think you'd like it much."

"How come?"

"It was kinda off-color."

Silas chewed on his lower lip. He wondered what Reuben's folks would have to say about that.

"How come ya don't give up this paintin' job and go back to helpin' your *daed* on the farm? I'm sure he could use the extra pair of hands, and—"

"I don't like farmin'," Reuben asserted. "In fact, there ain't much about the Amish ways I do like anymore."

Silas rocked back and forth on his heels, trying to think of the right thing to say. He'd been helping his pap work the land ever since he finished his eighth-grade education. That was seven years ago, and he was still happy staying at home. It didn't make sense to him that an Amish man, born and raised on a farm, preferred to be painting houses, stores, and the like.

"I'm sorry you feel thataway," Silas said. "Sure hope you're keepin' your opinions to yourself."

Reuben stopped painting and turned to face Silas. "What's that supposed to mean?"

Silas shrugged. "Bishop Weaver was at our place yesterday. He's heard some things, and he's gettin' mighty concerned."

"Things about me?"

Silas nodded. "Is it true?"

"Is what true?"

"That you have been runnin' around with some English fellows?"

Reuben's brows furrowed. "You plannin' on tellin' the bishop whatever I say to you now?"

"Himmel—no, no," Silas was quick to say. "I just thought I'd ask, that's all."

Reuben snorted. "All right then. . . *Jah,* I've done a few worldly things with some of the fellas I work with."

"Like what?"

Reuben shrugged. "Let's see now. . . We've gone to a couple of R-rated movies, had a few beers with our boss after work, and—"

Silas held up his hand. "Don'tcha know better than that? In Proverbs 23:20 it says, 'Be not among winebibbers.' And chapter six, verse fourteen of 2 Corinthians reminds us about not bein' unequally yoked with unbelievers."

"Yeah, I know all that, but I ain't no dummy. I've been readin' some books about other beliefs, and I'm not so sure I swallow all that Bible teachin' anymore."

"My pap told me once, 'Never mistake knowledge for wisdom. One might help you make a livin', but the other helps you make a life.' "

Reuben flicked a fly off his paintbrush and frowned. "Let's just say I've learned there's more to this world than sittin' in church for hours on end and followin' a bunch of silly rules. We only live once, and regardless of what your pap says, I aim to have me some fun!"

Hearing the way his friend was talking gave Silas a deep ache in his heart, just the way it had when he'd spoken with Anna yesterday. He didn't understand why so many of the *younga* were getting dissatisfied with the old ways. He closed his eyes and drew in a deep breath. He might not be able to do much about Reuben, but Anna was another matter. She needed him to intervene on her behalf, and if there was any way he could get her thinking straight again, he was determined to do it.

three

The following morning, Rachel awoke to the soothing sound of roosters crowing in the barnyard. She loved that noise—loved everything about their farm, in fact. She yawned, stretched, and squinted at the ray of sun peeking through a hole in her window shade. Today the family was planning to go to Farmers' Market, where they would sell some of their garden produce, as well as plants and flowers from Mom and Dad's greenhouse.

Dad, Joseph, and Perry were outside getting the larger market buggy ready when Rachel came downstairs to help with breakfast. The sweet smell of maple syrup greeted her as she entered the kitchen. Mom was mixing pancake batter, Anna was frying sausage and eggs, and Elizabeth was setting the table, which included a huge pitcher of fresh syrup.

"Gut Morgen," Rachel said cheerfully. "What can I do to help?"

Mom glanced up at Rachel, then back to the batter. "You can go outside and tell the *Mannsleit* we'll be ready with breakfast in ten minutes."

Rachel nodded, then made a hasty exit out the kitchen door. Dad and Perry were loading the back of their larger, four-sided market buggy, and Joseph was hitching the brawny horse that would pull it.

"Mom says breakfast in ten minutes," Rachel announced.

"You can go get washed up," Dad told Perry.

The young, freckle-faced boy pointed to the boxes of green beans sitting on the grass. "What about those?"

"You stay, and you go," Dad said, indicating his wish to

28

speak to Rachel alone. "I'll see to the boxes."

Perry straightened his twisted suspenders and took off on a run. From behind, his long legs made him appear much older than a boy of twelve. From the front, his impish grin and sparkling blue eyes made him look a child, full of life and laughter, mischief and fun.

Rachel stood quietly beside her father, waiting for him to speak. His shirtsleeves were rolled up to the elbows, and she marveled at how quickly his strong arms loaded the remaining boxes of beans. When the last box was put in place, Dad straightened and faced Rachel. "Do ya think you could do me a favor?"

Rachel twisted one corner of her apron and stared down at the ground. Dad's favors usually meant some kind of hard work. "I suppose so. What did ya have in mind?"

Dad bent down so he was eye-level with Rachel. "Well, now. . .I know how close you and Anna have always been. I was hopin' ya might let your *mamm* and me know what's goin' on with her these days."

Rachel opened her mouth to respond, but Dad cut her right off. "Fact of the matter is, Anna's been actin' mighty strange here of late, and we can't be sure we can trust her. We need your help findin' out what's up."

Rachel wrinkled her nose. Was Dad saying what she thought he was saying? Did he actually want her to spy on her sister? If Dad thought she and Anna were close, he was surely mistaken. Here of late, Rachel and Anna didn't see eye-to-eye on much of anything. Rachel knew if Anna's talk about learning more of the English ways ever reached Mom's or Dad's ears, they'd be plenty miffed. That was obvious by the way Dad had reacted last night when Anna mentioned they should modernize some. Rachel sure didn't want to be the one to tell them what was going on inside Anna's stubborn head.

"So, what do ya say?" Dad asked, pulling Rachel out of her troubling thoughts.

Rachel flicked her tongue across her dry lips. "What exactly am I expected to do?"

"To begin with, your *mamm's* been tellin' me that Anna has a suitor, yet she's not the least bit interested in courtin' the poor fellow."

"You must mean Silas Swartley," Rachel said with a frown. "He's sweet as molasses on Anna, but she won't give him the time of day." She shook her head. "Such a shame it is, too. Poor Silas is tryin' ever so hard to win her over."

Dad glanced toward the front of the market buggy, where Joseph was still hitching the horse. "Kinda reminds me of your *mamm* when I was tryin' to show her I cared."

Rachel listened politely as her father continued. "Sometimes a man shows his feelin's in a strange sort of way." Dad nodded toward Joseph and chuckled softly. "Now take that big brother of yours—we all know he's sweet on Pauline Hostetler, but do you think he'll do a thing about it? *Himmel.* . . Joseph's gonna fool around, and soon some other fellow's bound to come along and win her heart. Then it'll be too late for my boy."

Rachel knew all about Joseph's crush on Pauline. He'd been carrying a torch for Pauline ever since Eli Yoder dropped her to marry Laura, the fancy, English woman from Minnesota. The fact that Pauline was three years older than Joseph didn't help things, either. Rachel had to wonder if the age difference bothered Pauline the way it did her brother. It seemed rather strange that the twenty-four-year-old woman still wasn't married. Either she'd never gotten over Eli, or Pauline just wasn't interested in Joseph. He sure wasn't going to take the initiative, Rachel was pretty sure of that.

"Well, I'm thinkin' that if anyone can talk to Anna about givin' Silas a chance, it would be you," Dad said, cutting into

Rachel's contemplations one more time.

Rachel swallowed hard. *If Dad only knew what he was askin'. It's hard enough to see Silas hangin' around Anna all the time. How in the world can I be expected to talk Anna into somethin' she really don't wanna do?* Truth be told, Rachel would just as soon slop the hogs every day as to tell Anna how stupid she was for snubbing Silas.

She let her gaze travel over their orderly farmyard, then back to her father. *"Jah,* okay. I'll have a little talk with Anna 'bout Silas."

"And you'll tell us if anything strange is goin' on with your sister?"

Rachel nodded, feeling worse than pond scum in late August. "I'll tell."

❧

Farmers' Market was on the outskirts of Bird-in-Hand. It was only a twenty-minute ride from the Beachy farm, but today the trip seemed especially long. The cramped quarters in the buggy and the hot, sticky weather didn't help much, so Rachel was feeling kind of cross.

Dad and Mom rode in the front of the buggy, with Elizabeth sitting between them. There were two benches in back where Rachel, Anna, Joseph, and Perry sat. Behind them were the boxes filled with produce, plants, and fresh-cut flowers. Mom's wheelchair was scrunched in as well.

The temperature was in the nineties, with humidity so high Rachel could feel her damp dress and underclothes sticking to her body like flypaper. When they finally pulled into the graveled parking lot, she was the first to jump down from the buggy.

Perry tended to the horse, while Joseph and Dad unloaded the boxes and carried them inside the market building. Elizabeth and Rachel followed, with Anna a few feet behind, pushing Mom's wheelchair.

Everyone helped set up their table, and soon the Beachys were open for business. Whenever they were between customers, the children were allowed to take turns wandering around the market.

Rachel took a break around noontime and went to a stand where they were selling homemade ginger ale. A tall, gangly Amish fellow waited on her. He had freckles covering his nose and looked to be about nineteen or twenty. Rachel didn't recognize him and figured he must be from another district.

"It's a mighty hot day, ain't it so?" he asked, giving her a wide grin that revealed a mouthful of stained teeth.

Rachel had to wonder if the young man was among the Amish teenagers who liked to sow his wild oats. Could be that this fellow was hooked on cigarettes, which would explain the ugly yellow teeth. She thought it such a pity that so many of the *younga* became dissatisfied with their religion and wanted to see how the English lived. Her mind went immediately to her older sister. How she hoped Anna would never stoop so low as to start drinking and smoking, the way some in their district did. It would be a sin and a shame to waste her life that way.

Rachel smiled cordially at the man selling ginger ale. Even if he was sowing his oats, he still deserved to be treated with kindness. *"Jah,* it surely is warm," she said, handing him a fifty-cent piece. In return, he gave her a paper cup full of mouthwatering soda pop.

Rachel moved on to another table, where Nancy Frey, the schoolteacher who taught at the local Amish one-room schoolhouse, was selling a variety of pies.

Nancy smiled at Rachel. "Are ya here with your family?"

"Jah. We're sellin' produce and lots of flowers and plants from my folks' greenhouse," Rachel replied. "Our stand's at the other end of the building."

"I sure hope business is better for you than it has been

here. Pies aren't doin' so well today."

"That's too bad." Rachel licked her lips. "Yum! Apple-crumb, shoofly, and funny-cake are all my favorite pies."

Nancy laughed. "Would ya like to try a slice? I already have an apple-crumb cut."

"It's right temptin', but I'd better not spoil my appetite, or I won't be able to eat any of the lunch I brought along." She held up her cup of ginger ale. "Besides, I've got this to finish yet."

"How is your dear *mamm* these days?" Nancy asked. "Does she still get around on those crutches of hers?"

Rachel nodded. "She does some, though I think it's kinda hard for her to walk like a stiff-legged doll. She uses her wheelchair more often than the braces—probably because it's a mite easier."

"Jah, I can imagine."

"Well," Rachel said with a shrug, "guess I'll be movin' on. It's awful stuffy in here, so I think I'll step outside for a breath of what I hope will be fresh air."

Nancy nodded. "I know what ya mean. If I weren't here alone, I'd be goin' outside, too."

"I'd be more'n happy to watch your table," Rachel offered.

"Danki, but my sister, Emma, will probably be along soon. I'm sure she'll be willin' to let me take a little break."

"All right then." Rachel waved and moved away from Nancy's table, heading in the direction of the nearest exit.

Soon Rachel found the solace she was looking for under an enormous maple tree growing in the park right next to the market. She was about to take a seat at one of the picnic tables when she caught sight of Silas Swartley. Her heart slammed into her chest as she realized he was heading her way.

❧

Silas gritted his teeth. He'd just come from the Yutzys' table, and talking to Reuben's folks had made him feel downright sick. They knew what their son was up to. . .or at least some of it. Silas was pretty sure Reuben hadn't told them every-thing he was doing. But then, he hadn't really told Silas all that much.

Silas figured he should be minding his own business, but he couldn't stand by and watch two of his best friends get in trouble with the elders of the church for disobedience to the *Ordnung*. He knew Reuben was already doing some worldly things, but Anna was another matter. He was pretty sure she was only *thinking* on the idea. She was obviously dis-content with her life, but he was hoping to change all that. If Anna would agree to court him, then maybe he could per-suade her to give up all her silly notions about wanting to taste what the world had to offer.

Silas had come outside for a breath of fresh air and was headed over to the park when he noticed Anna's little sister Rachel. "Hmm. . .she might be just the one I need to talk to."

❧

Silas plunked down beside Rachel, without even bothering to ask if she minded or not. Of course, truth be told, it tickled her pink that he'd even want to be seen with her, much less sit right on the same bench.

"Whatcha doin' out here by yourself?" Silas asked as he took off his straw hat and began fanning his face with the brim.

"Tryin' to get cooled off," Rachel said, kind of breathless-like. For one wild moment, she had an impulse to lean her head on Silas's shoulder and confess her undying love for him. She didn't, of course, for she knew he would either be-come angry or laugh and call her a *kinder* who was much too young for someone as mature as him.

"I know what ya mean," Silas responded to her comment about the weather. "Whew! I thought it was hot inside, but I don't think it's a whole lot better out here."

So Silas had come from inside the market. *Funny thing,*

Rachel mused as her lips turned slightly upward. *I never saw him once all mornin'.* It was a surprise to her that Silas wasn't hanging around their table making googly eyes at Anna, the way he usually did.

"Rachel, I was wonderin' if we could talk," Silas said, breaking into her private thoughts.

"I thought we were talkin'."

He chuckled and dropped his hat to his knees. "*Jah,* I guess we were at that. What I really meant to say was, can we talk about your sister?"

Rachel's smile turned upside down. She might have known Silas hadn't planned to talk about her. She shrugged, trying not to let her disappointment show. "What about Anna? It was *that* sister you were referrin' to, right?"

Silas shifted his gaze toward the sky. "Of course I meant Anna. It sure enough couldn't be Elizabeth. I ain't no cradle robber, ya know."

Rachel felt as though Silas had slapped her right across the face. Even though he was speaking about her twelve-year-old sister, she still got his meaning. She knew Silas wouldn't dream of looking at her, since she was five years younger and all. Besides, what chance did she have against the beauty of her older sister? She stared off into space, hoping he wouldn't notice the tears that had gathered in her eyes.

In a surprise gesture, Silas touched Rachel's chin and turned her head so she was looking directly at him. Her chest fluttered with the sensation of his touch, and it was all she could do to keep from falling right off the bench. "So, what is it ya wanted to say 'bout Anna?" she asked with a catch in her voice.

"You and your sister are pretty close, ain't it so?"

She gulped and tried to regain her composure. "I used to think so."

"Anna probably talks more to you than anyone else, right?"

Rachel shook her head. "I think she tells her friend Martha Rose a whole lot more'n she tells me."

Silas lifted one eyebrow in question. "Martha Rose?"

Rachel nodded. "Yep. They have been *gut* friends for a long time."

Several seconds went by before Silas spoke again. "Hmm. . . I suppose I could talk to Martha Rose, but I don't know her all that well. I'd feel a might more comfortable talkin' to you 'bout Anna than I would her best friend."

Rachel supposed she should have been flattered that Silas would want to avail her as a confidant, yet the thought of him only using her to learn more about Anna irked her to no end.

"Okay," she finally conceded, "what do you wanna know 'bout my sister?"

"Can you tell me how to make her pay me some mind?" Silas asked, looking ever so serious. "I've tried everything but stand on my head and wiggle my ears, yet still, she treats me like yesterday's dirty laundry. I tell you, Rachel, it's got me plumb worn out tryin' to get sweet Anna to court me."

Sweet Anna? Rachel thought ruefully. *Silas, you might not think my sister's so sweet if you knew all the things she's been sayin'. . .about you and the Amish way of life.*

Rachel felt sorry for poor Silas, sitting here all woebegone, pining for her sister's attention. If she wasn't so crazy about the fellow herself, she might pitch in and try to set things right between him and Anna. With a slight shrug, she responded to Silas's question. "I think only God can get my sister thinkin' straight again." She looked away, studying a row of trees on the other side of the park.

"You're kinda pensive today," Silas noted. "Is it this oppressive heat, or are ya just not wantin' to help me with Anna?"

Rachel tipped her head forward, the whole while praying for something to say that wouldn't be a lie and wouldn't hurt Silas's feelings. Finally, she lifted her chin and faced him again. "I think a man who claims to care for a woman should speak on his own behalf. Even though Anna and I don't talk much anymore, I still know her fairly well, and I don't think Anna would like it if she knew you were plottin' like this."

Silas twisted his hands together. "I ain't plottin, Rachel. I'm just tryin' to figure out some way to make Anna commit to courtin' me, that's all. I thought maybe you could help out, but if you're gonna get all peevish on me, then just forget I even brought up the subject."

Now I've gone and done it. Silas will never come to care for me if I keep on makin' him mad. Rachel placed her trembling hand on Silas's bare arm, and the sudden contact with his skin caused her hand to feel like it was on fire. "Maybe it wouldn't hurt if I had a little talk with Anna."

A huge grin spread across Silas's handsome face. "You mean it, Rachel? You'd really go to bat for me?"

She nodded slowly, feeling like she was one of her father's old sows being led away to slaughter. First she'd promised Dad to help Anna and Silas get together, and now she was promising Silas to speak to Anna on his behalf. It made no sense, since she didn't really want them to be together. But a promise was a promise, so she smiled and said, *"Jah,* I'll do my best."

four

It was Sunday morning, and church was to be held at eight-thirty, in the home of Eli and Laura Yoder. They only lived a few farms away from the Beachys, so the horse and buggy ride didn't take long at all.

Many buggies were parked near the side of the Yoders' house, but Dad managed to find an empty spot on the side where Eli's folks' addition had been built. Joseph helped Mom into her wheelchair, then everyone else climbed out and scattered, hoping to find friends and relatives to visit with during their free time before church started.

Rachel noticed Silas Swartley standing on one end of the front porch, and she silently berated herself for loving him. She was almost certain he would never love her in return. She wasn't sure he even liked her. *I either need to put him out of my mind or figure out some way to make him take notice of me.*

Silas seemed to be focused on Anna, who was talking with her friends Martha Rose Zook and Laura Yoder at the other end of the porch. *Guess I'd better speak to Anna soon, before Silas comes askin' if I did.* Rachel joined her sister and the other two women, but made sure she was standing close enough to Anna so she could whisper into her ear. "Look," she said softly, "there's Silas Swartley. He seems to be watchin' you."

Anna shrugged. "So?"

"Don'tcha think he's good-lookin'?"

Anna nudged Rachel in the ribs. "Since you seem so interested, why not go over and talk to him?"

Rachel gasped. "I could never do that!"

"Why not?"

"It's you he's interested in, not me."

"I think we'd better hurry and get inside. Preachin's about to begin," Anna said, conveniently changing the subject.

Rachel followed her sister into the Yoders' living room, where several rows of backless, wooden benches were set up. She'd have to try speaking to Anna about Silas later on.

The men and boys took their seats on one side of the room and the women and girls on the other. Rachel sat between her two sisters, with Mom sitting in her wheelchair at the end of their bench, closest to Elizabeth.

All whispering ceased, as the hymnals were passed out by one of the deacons. In singsong, almost chantlike voices, the congregation recited several traditional Dutch hymns. Next, one of the ministers delivered a short message, followed by a longer sermon by Bishop Weaver.

Rachel noticed that Elizabeth was fidgeting, obviously growing restless. Mom reached over and placed a firm hand on the child's knee. "Sit still," she whispered. "Even the little ones like David Yoder and his baby sister aren't fussin', so you shouldn't be neither."

"I'm hungry," Elizabeth whined. "When's church gonna be over?"

Mom gave her a cross look. "You're not too old for a visit to the woodshed, ya know."

Elizabeth sat up straight and never gave another word of complaint.

The next hour was spent in silent prayer and Bible reading. Rachel glanced over at Anna. She was twiddling her thumbs and staring out the window.

What's that willful sister of mine thinkin' about? Rachel had a terrible feeling that Anna's curiosity over worldly things and her dissatisfaction with their Old Order ways would only lead to trouble. What if Anna were to up and leave the faith?

Rachel clenched her teeth. *No, that can't happen. It would break Mom's and Dad's hearts, not to mention upsettin' the whole family. Why, we'd have to shun our own flesh and blood!* Rachel shuddered just thinking about it. Right then, she vowed to pray more, asking the Lord to change her sister's mind about things. She would even make herself be happy about Anna and Silas courting if it meant Anna would alter her attitude and be happy being Amish.

Rachel felt a sense of relief when the preaching service was finally over. It wasn't that she didn't enjoy church, but all those troubling thoughts rolling around in her head were enough to make her feel downright miserable.

Outside in the front yard, several large tables were set up, and soon each of them was laden with an abundance of tasty food. There were large platters of roast beef, bowls of mashed potatoes, bread stuffing, pickled red beets, hot cabbage slaw, fresh cucumbers, steamed brown bread, butter, apple jelly, pitchers of cool milk, and for dessert, tart cherry pie, topped with homemade vanilla ice cream.

Rachel and Anna joined several other young women as they began to serve the menfolk. After that, the women and children took their places at separate tables.

When the meal was over and everything had been cleared away, men and women of all ages gathered in small groups to visit. The younger children were put down to nap, while the older ones started playing games of hide-and-seek, tag, and corner-ball. The young adults also gathered. Some joined the games, while others were content to just sit and talk.

Rachel didn't feel much like playing games or engaging in idle chitchat, so she decided to take a walk. Walking always seemed to help her relax and think more clearly. She left Anna talking with a group of women and headed off in the direction of the small pond near the end of the Yoders' alfalfa field.

The pool of clear water was surrounded by low-hanging

willow trees, offering shade and solitude on another hot, sticky day in July. Feeling the heat bear down on her, Rachel slipped off her shoes and socks, then waded along the water's edge, relishing the way the cool water tickled her toes. When she felt somewhat cooler, she plunked down on the grass. Closing her eyes, Rachel found herself thinking about the meeting she'd had with Silas the day before. She'd only made one feeble attempt to talk to Anna about him and knew she really should try again. It was the least she could do, since she had made a promise.

A snapping twig caused Rachel to jump. She jerked her head in the direction of the sound and was surprised to see Silas standing under one of the willow trees. He smiled and winked at her. It made her heart beat faster and was just enough to rekindle her hope that he might actually forget about Anna and come to love her instead.

"I didn't know anyone else was here," Rachel murmured as Silas moved over to where she was sitting.

"I didn't know anyone was here, either." Silas removed his straw hat and plopped down on the grass beside her. They relaxed in silence for a time, listening to the rhythmic birdsong filtering through the trees and an occasional *ribbet* from a noisy bullfrog.

Rachel thought about all the times Silas had visited their farm. She remembered one day in particular when a baby robin had fallen from its nest in the giant maple. Silas had climbed that old tree like it was nothing, then put the tiny creature back in its home. That was the day Rachel gave her heart to Silas Swartley. Too bad he didn't know it.

"I just talked to Reuben Yutzy," Silas said, breaking into Rachel's private thoughts. "He's been workin' for a paint contractor in Lancaster for some time now."

She nodded but made no comment.

"Reuben informed me that he's leavin' the Amish faith."

Silas slowly shook his head. "Can you believe it, Rachel? Reuben's been my friend since we were *kinder,* and now our friendship is gonna be over."

Rachel's mouth dropped open. "I'd never have guessed Reuben would leave. I always thought he was settled into our ways. As I recall, he never even joined his brothers when they decided to sow their wild oats."

The lines in Silas's forehead deepened. "Well, he's sowin' them now. Since he started workin' for that English man, Reuben's been hangin' around the wrong crowd and doin' all sorts of worldly things. I tried talkin' to him the other day, but I guess nothin' I said got through his thick skull. Reuben's made up his mind about leavin', and he seems bent on followin' that path."

"Many of our men work in town for paint contractors, carpenters, and other tradesmen," Rachel reminded. "Most of them remain in the faith in spite of their jobs."

"I know, but like I said, Reuben got mixed up with the wrong sort of English folks." Silas gave his earlobe a few tugs. "Reuben told me that he bought a fancy truck awhile back, but he's been keepin' it parked outside his boss's place of business so none of his family would know."

Rachel fidgeted with her hands. She wanted so badly to reach out and touch Silas's disheartened face. It would feel so right to smooth the wrinkles out of his forehead. She released a deep sigh instead. "Things are sure gettin' *verhuddelt* here of late."

Silas nodded. "You're right about things bein' mixed up. I think there's somethin' else goin' on with Reuben, too."

"Like what?"

"I'm not sure. He dropped a few hints, but when I pressed him about it, he closed up like a snail crawlin' into its shell. Said he didn't want to talk about it." Silas grimaced. "I'm thinkin' maybe there's a woman involved."

"An Englisher?"

"Might could be. It wouldn't be the first time an Amish man fell for an English gal." Silas shrugged. "That's what happened to Eli Yoder a few years back, ya know."

Rachel nodded. *"Jah,* but Laura joined the Amish faith, so Eli never was shunned." She pulled a hanky from her apron pocket, dried her bare feet on it, then slipped her socks and shoes back on before she stood up. "I should be gettin' back to the house. My folks are likely to miss me, and they'll probably send Joseph out lookin'." She shook her head. "I'm not in any mood to deal with my cranky brother today."

"Joseph's not happy?"

"Nope. He's got a big crush on Pau—" Rachel's hand flew to her mouth when she realized she'd almost let something slip. "Like as I was sayin'," she mumbled, "I need to head back."

"Wait!" Silas jumped to his feet. "I was wonderin' if you've had a chance to speak with Anna yet."

Rachel felt her cheeks flame as she turned to face him. She worried that he might be able to see right through her. Could Silas possibly be reading her mind? She hoped not, because she really didn't want him to know what she was thinking right now.

"Silas, I still believe it would be best if you spoke with her yourself." Rachel touched his arm lightly. "And my advice is, you'd better do it soon, before it's too late."

❧

Rachel and her family were packing up to leave the Yoders' place when she noticed Silas had Anna cornered next to his courting buggy. Her sister didn't look any too happy about it, and Rachel could only wonder why. She inched a bit closer, hoping to catch a word or two. Eavesdropping was becoming a habit, it seemed, but she didn't seem able to help herself. Besides, it wasn't like she was doing it on purpose. People just seemed to be in the wrong place at the wrong time.

"I think it would be best if you'd forget about me," she heard Anna say. "Ya really should find someone more suited to you."

Silas shuffled his feet a few times, turning his hat over and over in his hands. "Don't rightly think there's anyone more suited to me, Anna."

Anna shrugged. "If ya think about it, you'll realize that we don't have much in common. Never have, really. On the other hand, I know who would be just right for you."

Me. . .me. . . Rachel squeezed her eyes shut, waiting to hear Silas's next words.

"Who might that be?" he asked.

"Rachel."

"Don't start with that again, Anna."

Rachel's eyes snapped open. She had to give up this silly game of bouncing back and forth from hope to despair. It only proved her immaturity, which was exactly why Silas saw her as a mere child.

"She likes a lot of the same things you like, Silas," her sister asserted. "Besides, I think she's crazy about you." Anna nodded toward her family's buggy, where Rachel stood, dumbfounded and unable to move. She'd probably never be able to look Silas in the face again.

Silas didn't seem to even notice her, for he was looking straight at Anna. "As I've said before, Rachel's not much more'n a *kinder*. I need someone who's mature enough for marriage and ready to settle down."

"Rachel is eighteen, soon to be nineteen," Anna said, emphasizing the words. "Give her a few more months, and she'll be about the right age for marryin'."

"But, it's you I love, Anna." Silas's tone was pleading, and if Rachel hadn't been so angry at her sister for embarrassing her, she might have felt pity for the man she loved.

"Rachel, are ya gettin' in or not?" Dad's booming voice

jerked Rachel around to face him.

"What about Anna? She's still talkin' to Silas over by his buggy." Rachel pointed in that direction, but Dad merely grabbed up the reins.

"I'm sure Silas will see that Anna gets home," Mom put in. "After all, you did mention that he's sweet on her."

Rachel's throat ached from holding back tears, and she reached up to massage her throbbing temples. Silas thought she was just a *kinder,* and he was in love with Anna. At the rate things were going, she might never get to use her hope chest. She glanced Silas's way one last time, then hopped into the buggy and took her seat at the rear.

"Why are you lookin' so down in the mouth?" Joseph asked.

She folded her arms and scowled. "It is none of your business."

"I'll bet she'll tell me," Elizabeth piped up. "I'm a girl, and girls only share their deepest secrets with another girl. Ain't that right, Sister?"

Before Rachel could answer, Perry put in his two cents worth. "Aw, Rachel's probably got a bee in her *Kapp* 'cause she don't have a steady boyfriend yet. She's most likely jealous of Anna gettin' to ride home with Silas Swartley." He gave Rachel an impish smile. "That's it, ain't it? You're green with envy, huh?"

"Leave Rachel alone," Mom hollered back. "If she wants to talk about whatever's botherin' her, she will. Now, let's see how quiet we can make the rest of this ride home."

five

The following day, Rachel felt more fretful than ever. She'd hardly said more than two words to anyone all morning and was sorely tempted to tell Anna she'd overheard most of her conversation with Silas yesterday. In fact, she was working up her courage and praying for just the right words as she hung a batch of laundry on the line.

Anna came out of the greenhouse and headed in Rachel's direction. *Guess this is as good a time as any,* Rachel decided. She waved and called her sister to come over. Anna merely waved back and kept right on walking toward the barn. A short time later, she emerged with one of the driving horses, then began to hitch the mare to the buggy.

"Where are ya goin'?" Rachel asked, dropping one of Perry's shirts into the wicker basket and moving toward Anna.

"Gotta run some errands in town, then I may stop by and see Martha Rose for a bit."

"You be careful now," Mom called. She was sitting on the front porch in her wheelchair, shelling peas into an bowl.

"I will," Anna hollered as she stepped into the buggy.

"And don't be out too late, neither," Mom added. "There was a bad accident last week along the main highway. It was gettin' dark, and the car driver didn't see the horse and buggy in time."

"I'll be careful." Anna flicked the reins, and the horse and buggy were soon out of sight.

Rachel bent down and snatched a pair of Dad's trousers from the wicker basket. "Guess I'll have to catch Anna later," she grumbled.

"Rachel!" Mom called.

"*Jah?*"

"When you're done with the laundry, I'd like ya to go over to the greenhouse and help your *daed*. I've got several things here at the house needin' to be done, so I won't be able to work out there today."

"What about Anna? She's the one who likes workin' with flowers."

"She's runnin' errands in Paradise."

Rachel already knew that. What she didn't know was why. Couldn't *she* have gone to town so Anna could have kept working in the greenhouse? Life wasn't always fair, but she knew there was no point in arguing. Rachel cupped her hands around her mouth. "*Jah,* okay, Mom! I'll go over to the greenhouse as soon as I'm done here."

❧

Silas's morning chores were done, but he had a few errands to run for Pap. He decided this would be a good time to stop by the Beachys' greenhouse and have a little talk with Anna. Maybe he'd even buy Mom a new indoor plant or something she could put out in her garden. That would give him a good excuse for stopping at Grandma's Place, and it might keep Anna from suspecting the real reason for his visit.

Half an hour later, Silas stepped inside the greenhouse and was surprised to see Rachel sitting behind the counter, writing something on a tablet. "*Gut Morgen,*" he said, offering her a smile. "Is Anna about?"

She shook her head. "Nope. Just me and my *daed* are here today." She motioned toward the back room. "He's repottin' several African violets that have outgrown their containers."

Silas's smile turned upside down. "I thought Anna usually worked in the greenhouse. She ain't sick, I hope."

Rachel tapped her pencil along the edge of the counter. "She went to Paradise. Had some errands to run."

Silas scratched the back of his head. "Hmm. . .guess maybe

I can try to catch up with her there. I have some errands to run today, too." He turned toward the door, all thoughts of buying a plant forgotten. If he hurried, he might make it to Paradise in time to find Anna there. The town wasn't very big, so if she was still running errands, he was bound to spot her. "Have a nice day. See ya later, Rachel," Silas called over his shoulder.

☙

Anna. . .Anna. . .Anna, Rachel fumed. *Is that all Silas ever thinks about? He didn't bother to ask how I was doing or even make small talk about the weather.*

"I heard the bell ring above the door," Dad said as he entered the room. "Did we have a customer, or where ya just checking to see how things look outside?"

Rachel was about to answer, when she felt a sneeze coming on. She grabbed a hanky out of her apron pocket, leaned her head back, and let out a big *ker-choo!*

"Bless you, Child."

"Danki."

"You're not comin' down with a summer cold, I hope," Dad said, giving her a look of concern.

She shook her head. "I think I'm allergic to all these flowers. I do okay with the ones growing outside, but bein' cooped with 'em is a whole different matter."

"Guess workin' in the greenhouse isn't your idea of fun, huh?"

She turned her head away and mumbled, "Truth is, I would rather be outside."

Making no mention of her preference, Dad asked, "How come the doorbell jingled and we have no customers?"

"It was Silas Swartley," Rachel replied. "He was lookin' for Anna, and when I told him she was runnin' errands in Paradise, he hightailed it outta here, lickety-split."

Dad chuckled. "Ah, love is in the air; there's no doubt about it."

Rachel nibbled on the end of her pencil, remembering the way Silas looked whenever he spoke of Anna. It made her sick to her stomach, knowing Anna didn't love Silas in return.

Dad grinned like an old hound dog. "Someday your time will come, Rachel. Just be patient and have hope that God will send the right man your way."

❧

It was after nine o'clock, and still Anna hadn't returned home. Dad and Mom were sitting on the front porch, talking about their workday and doing a bit of worrying over their eldest daughter, while Rachel kept Elizabeth entertained with a game of checkers on the little table at one end of the porch. Joseph and Perry were out in the barn, grooming the horses and cleaning Joseph's courting buggy.

Rachel had just kinged her last red checker and was about to ask her little sister if she wanted to give up the game and have another piece of funny-cake pie when a horse and buggy came up the graveled drive. It was Anna, and before she even got the horse reined in, Dad was on his feet.

"Why are you so late, Daughter?" he called as he ran toward the buggy. "You sure couldn't have been runnin' errands all this time."

The porch was bathed in light from several kerosene lanterns, but the night sky was almost dark. Rachel knew Anna wasn't supposed to be out after the sun went down because there was too much risk of an accident, even with the battery-operated lights on the buggy.

Rachel peered across the yard and strained to hear what Anna and their father were saying. *Sure hope that sister of mine hasn't done anything foolish today.* An unsettled feeling slid through Rachel as she watched Anna step from the buggy.

"Your *mamm* and me were gettin' mighty worried," Dad's deep voice announced.

Mom coasted down the wheelchair ramp. "Oh, thank the

Lord! I'm so glad to see you're safe!"

"Sorry. I didn't realize that it was gettin' so late," Anna apologized.

"Well, you're home now, and that's what counts," Dad said. "We can talk about where you've been so long after I get the horse and buggy put away." He quickly unhitched the mare and led her off toward the barn.

"Anna, where's your apron and *Kapp?*" Mom asked as Anna stepped in front of the wheelchair.

Rachel studied her sister closely. Sure enough, Anna wasn't wearing anything over her dark blue cotton dress. No cape. No apron. No head covering! What in the world was that girl thinking?

Anna glanced down at her dress. "I–uh–guess I must have left it somewhere."

"Genesis 3:7!" Elizabeth hollered. " 'And they sewed fig leaves together, and made themselves aprons.' Ain't that what the Bible says? Ain't that why Amish women wear *Kapps* and aprons?"

Anna shot Elizabeth a look that could have stopped the old key-wound clock in the parlor, but she pushed past her little sister and started to open the front screen door without any comeback.

"Wait a minute, Anna." Mom propelled herself back up the ramp. "We need to talk about this, don'tcha think?"

Anna shrugged. "Can't it wait 'til tomorrow? I'm kinda tired."

Rachel gulped. If Anna were a few years younger, she'd have had a switch taken to her backside for talking to their mother that way. What in the world had come over her?

"It may be gettin' late, and you might be tired, but this is a serious matter and it won't wait 'til tomorrow," Mom asserted.

Anna pointed at Rachel, then Elizabeth. "Can't we talk someplace else? No use bringin' the whole family into this."

Mom folded her arms and set her lips in a straight line,

indicating her intent to hold firm. "Maybe your sisters can learn somethin' from this discussion. I think it would be a *gut* idea if they stay—at least 'til your *daed* returns. Then we'll let him decide."

Rachel sucked in a deep breath and held it while she waited to see what Anna's next words would be.

"Guess I don't have much say in this," Anna said, dropping to the porch swing with a groan.

"Are ya gonna make your next move?" Elizabeth asked Rachel. "I just took one of your kings while you were starin' off into space."

Rachel jerked her thoughts back to the checkerboard. "I don't see how you managed that. . .unless you were cheatin'. I *was* winnin' this game, ya know."

Elizabeth thrust out her chin. "I wasn't cheatin'!"

Rachel was planning to argue the point further, but the sound of her father's heavy boots on the steps drew her attention away from the game again.

"Joseph's tendin' the horse," Dad said, looking down at Anna, who was pumping the swing back and forth like there was no tomorrow. "Now, are ya ready to tell us where you've been all day?" A muscle in Dad's cheek began to twitch, and Rachel knew it wasn't a good sign.

"Why aren't ya wearin' your apron and *Kapp,* Anna?" he shouted.

Rachel flinched, right along with her older sister. Their father didn't often get angry, but when he was mad enough to holler like that, everyone knew they'd better listen.

"I—uh. . ." Anna hung her head. "Can't we talk about this later?"

Dad slapped his hands together, and everyone, including Mom, jumped like a bullfrog. "We'll talk about it now!"

Anna's chin began to quiver. "Dad, couldn't I speak to you and Mom in private?"

He glanced down at Mom, who had wheeled her chair right next to the swing. "What do you think, Rebekah?"

She shrugged. "I guess it might be best." She turned her chair around so she was facing Rachel and Elizabeth. "You two had better clear away the game. It's about time to get washed up and ready for bed anyway."

"But, Mama," Elizabeth argued. "I'm almost ready to skunk Rachel and—"

Rachel shook her head. "Do as Mom says. You can skunk me some other time." She grabbed up the checkerboard, let the pieces fall into her apron, folded it up, then turned toward the front door. As curious as she was about where Anna had been and why she was dressed in such a manner, Rachel knew it was best to obey her parents. She'd have a heart-to-heart talk with her rebellious sister tomorrow morning. Until then, she'd be doing a whole lot of praying!

❧

Mom and Anna were preparing breakfast when Rachel came downstairs the following morning. "You're late," Anna complained. She was stirring the oatmeal so hard, Rachel feared it would come flying right out of the pot.

"How do you think you're gonna run a house of your own if ya can't be more reliable?" Anna continued to fume.

"Anna Beachy, just because you got up on the wrong side of the bed, it don't give ya just call to be *gridlich* with your sister this mornin'," Mom scolded. She was sitting at the kitchen table, buttering a huge stack of toast, and the look on her face told Rachel that her mother would not tolerate anyone being cranky this morning.

Rachel hurried to set the table, knowing it would be best to keep quiet.

Anna brought the kettle of oatmeal to the table and plopped it on a pot holder, nearly spilling the contents. "Like as not, you'll be gettin' married someday, Rachel, and I was wonderin' if you'd care to have my hope chest."

Rachel glanced at her mother, but Mom merely shrugged and continued buttering the toast. Anna was sure acting funny. Of course, she'd been acting pretty strange for several weeks now. Rachel could hardly wait until breakfast was over and she had a chance to corner Anna for a good talk. She was dying to know where her sister had been last night and what had happened during her little discussion with their folks.

"I've already got a start on my own hope chest, but thanks anyways," Rachel said, giving Anna the briefest of smiles.

"I'd sure like to go to Emma Troyer's today," Mom said, changing the subject. "She's feelin' kind of poorly and could probably use some help with laundry and whatnot." She sighed deeply. "Trouble is, I've got too much of my own things needin' to be done here and out at the greenhouse."

"I'll go," Anna said as she went to the refrigerator and took out a pitcher of milk.

Mom nodded. "If ya don't dally and come straight home, then I suppose it'd be all right. You'll hafta wait 'til this afternoon, though. I need help bakin' pies this mornin'."

Rachel could hardly believe her ears. Wasn't Anna in any kind of trouble for coming home late last night and not wearing her *Kapp* and apron? What sort of story had she fed the folks so that Mom would allow her to take the buggy out again today? Worse yet, if Anna went gallivanting off, it would probably mean Rachel would be asked to help in the greenhouse for the second day in a row. She had planned to do some bird-watching this afternoon, and maybe, if there were enough time, she would go fishing at the river. From the way things looked, she'd most likely be working all day.

"Did I hear someone mention pies?" Elizabeth asked excitedly. Rachel hadn't even noticed her younger sister enter the room. She'd been too upset over Anna's request to leave the farm again.

"I sure hope you're plannin' to make a raspberry cream pie, 'cause you know it's my favorite!" Elizabeth went on.

Mom gave the child a little pat on the backside when she sidled up to the table. "If you're willin' to help Perry pick raspberries, it might could be that we'll do up a few of your favorite pies." Her forehead wrinkled slightly. "Our raspberry bushes are loaded this summer, and if they're not picked soon, the berries are liable to fall clean off. Now that would surely be a waste, don'tcha think?"

Elizabeth's lower lip came jutting out. "I don't like to pick berries with Perry. He always throws the green berries at me."

"I'll have a little talk with your twin brother 'bout that," Mom stated. "Now, run outside and call the *Mannsleit* in for breakfast."

Rachel was glad when the morning meal was over. Anna had gone out to feed the hogs, and Rachel was on her way to gather eggs in the henhouse. Maybe they could finally find time for that little chat she'd been waiting to have.

With basket in hand, Rachel started across the yard, wishing she could go for a long walk. The scent of green grass kissed by early morning dew and the soft call of a dove caused a stirring in her heart. There was no time for a walk or even lingering in the yard. Rachel had chores to do, and she'd best get to them.

A short time later, Rachel reached under a fat hen and retrieved a plump, brown egg. A few more like that and she'd soon have the whole basket filled. When she finished, there were ten chunky eggs in the basket, and several cranky hens pecking and fussing at Rachel for disturbing their nests.

"You critters hush now," she scolded. "We need these eggs a heap more'n you, so shoo!" Rachel waved her hands, and the hens all scattered.

When an orange-and-white barn cat brushed against Rachel's leg and began to purr, she placed the basket on a bale of straw and plopped down next to it. Rachel enjoyed all the barnyard critters. They seemed so content with their lot in life. Not like one *person* she knew.

"What am I gonna do, Whiskers?" Rachel whispered. "I'm in love with someone, and he don't even know I'm alive. All he thinks about is my older sister." Her eyes drifted shut as an image of Silas Swartley flooded her mind. She could see him standing in the meadow, holding his straw hat in one hand and running the other hand through his dark chestnut hair. She imagined herself in the scene, walking slowly toward Silas with her arms outstretched.

"Sleepin' on the job, are ya?"

Rachel's eyes popped open, and she snapped her head in the direction of the deep male voice that had pulled her out of her reverie. "Joseph, you 'bout scared me to death, sneakin' up thataway."

He chuckled. "I wasn't really sneakin', but I sure thought you'd gone off to sleep there in your chair of straw." He sat down beside her. "What were you thinkin' about, anyways?"

Rachel gave Joseph's hat a little yank so it drooped down over his eyes. "I'll never tell."

Joseph righted his hat and jabbed her in the ribs with his elbow. "Like as not, it's probably some fellow you've got on your mind. My guess is maybe you and Anna have been bit by the summer love bug."

Rachel frowned deeply. "What do you know 'bout Anna? Has she told ya she's in love with someone?"

Joseph leaned over to stroke the cat's head, for Whiskers was now rubbing against *his* leg. "She hasn't said nothin' to me personally, but she's been actin' mighty strange here lately. I hear tell she got in pretty late last night, and there's been other times when Anna's whereabouts haven't been accounted for. What other reason could she have for actin' so secretive, unless some man's involved?"

Rachel remembered Silas saying he was going to Paradise yesterday and hoped to find Anna. Could she possibly have spent the day with him? She grabbed the basket of eggs and jumped up. "I've gotta get these back to the house. See ya later, Joseph!"

Rachel tore out of the barn and dashed toward the hog pen, where she hoped to find Anna still feeding the sow and her new brood of piglets. In her hurry, she tripped over a rock and nearly fell flat on her face. "*Ach,* my!" she complained. "The last thing I need this mornin' is to break all the eggs I've gathered."

She walked a little slower, but disappointment flooded her soul when she saw that Anna wasn't at the pigpen. Rachel had to wonder if she'd already left for Emma Troyer's.

Back at the house, Rachel was relieved to see Mom, Anna, and Elizabeth rolling out pie dough at the kitchen table. Each held a wooden rolling pin, and Rachel noticed that Elizabeth had more flour on her clothes than she did on the heavy piece of muslin cloth used as a rolling mat.

"You're just in time," Mom said with a nod of her head. "Why don't ya add some sugar to the bowl of raspberries on the cupboard over there?"

Rachel put the eggs in the refrigerator, then went to the sink to wash her hands. "Elizabeth, it sure didn't take you and Perry long to pick those berries. How'd ya get done so fast?"

"Mama helped," Elizabeth replied. "Her wheelchair fits fine between the rows, and she can pick faster'n anybody I know!"

Mom chuckled. "When you've had as many years' practice as me, you'll be plenty fast, too."

Rachel glanced at Anna. She was rolling her piecrust real hard—like she was taking her frustrations out on that clump of sticky dough. Rachel figured this probably wasn't a good time to be asking her sister any questions. Besides the fact that Anna seemed a might testy, Mom and Elizabeth were there. It didn't take a genius to know Anna wouldn't be about to bare her soul in front of them.

Rachel reached for a bag of sugar on the top shelf of the cupboard. She'd have to wait awhile yet. . .until she had Anna all to herself.

The pie baking was finished a little before noon, and Anna, who seemed right anxious to be on her way, asked if she could forego lunch and head over to Emma's.

"*Jah*, I suppose that'd be okay," Mom said. "I could fix ya a sandwich to eat on the way."

Anna waved her hand. "Don't trouble yourself. I'm sure Emma will have somethin' for me to eat."

Mom nodded but sent Anna off with a basket of fresh fruit and a jug of freshly made iced tea. "For Emma," she stated.

Rachel finished wiping down the table, then excused herself to go outside, hoping her sister hadn't left yet. She saw Anna hitching the horse to the buggy, but just when she was about to call out to her, Dad came running across the yard. "Not so late tonight, Anna!"

Anna climbed into the buggy. "I'll do my best to be back before dark."

Dad stepped aside, and the horse moved forward.

Rachel's heart sank. *Not again! Am I ever gonna get the chance to speak with that sister of mine?* With a sigh of resignation, she turned and headed back to the house. Today was not going one bit as planned!

six

Rachel gripped the front porch railing, watching as Anna climbed out of the buggy and began to unhitch the horse. It was almost dark. She could hardly believe Anna would be so brazen as to disobey their parents two nights in a row. *What kind of shenanigan is Anna pullin' now?*

Before Rachel had a chance to say anything to her sister, Dad was at Anna's side, taking the reins from her. "Late again," he grumbled. "You know right well we don't like ya out after dark." He shook his finger in her face. "You'd better have a good excuse for this, Daughter. Somethin' better'n what ya told us last night."

Rachel wanted to holler out, "What did ya tell them last night?" Instead, she just stood there like a statue, waiting to hear Anna's reply.

Anna hung her head. "I—uh—need to have a little heart-to-heart talk with you and Mom."

"Fine. I'll do up the horse, then meet ya inside." Dad walked away, and Anna stepped onto the porch. She drew Rachel into her arms.

"What was that for?" Rachel asked. A feeling of bewilderment, mixed with mounting fear, crept into her soul.

Anna's eyes glistened with tears. "No matter what happens, always remember that I love you."

Rachel's forehead wrinkled. "What's goin' on, Anna? Are you in some kinda trouble?"

Anna's only response was a deep sigh.

"I've been wantin' to talk to you all day—to see why you have been actin' so strange—and to find out how come you were late last night."

Anna drew in a shuddering breath. "Guess you'll learn it soon enough, 'cause I'm about to tell Dad and Mom the truth about where I was then and tonight."

"Weren't ya runnin' errands in Paradise yesterday?"

Anna shook her head.

"And today—did ya spend the day at Emma Troyer's?"

"I went to Lancaster—both times," Anna admitted as she sank into a rocking chair on the front porch. "I know you probably won't understand this, but I'm gonna have to leave the faith."

Rachel's mouth dropped open. "Oh, no. . .that just can't be! How could ya even think of doin' such a thing?"

A pathetic groan escaped Anna's lips and she began to cry.

Rachel knelt in front of the rocker and grasped her sister's trembling hand. "I'm guessin' the folks don't know," she said, hoping this was some kind of a crazy mistake and that as soon as Anna was thinking straight again, she'd make it all right.

"I made up some story about why I was late last night. I said I was with Silas all day, and the reason I wasn't wearin' my apron was because I spilled ice cream down the front of it."

"And the *Kapp?*" Rachel questioned. "How come ya weren't wearin' that last night?"

Anna winced, as though she'd been slapped. "I lied about that, too. Said Silas wanted to see me with my hair down, so I took it off and forgot to put it back on before I headed home."

Rachel's mind was whirling like Mom's gas-powered washing machine running at full speed. First Anna had said she wasn't interested in Silas, then she'd lied and said she was. It made no sense at all. The words she wanted to speak stuck in her throat like a wad of chewing gum.

"You—you—really lied to the folks about all that?" she squeaked.

Anna nodded.

"And they believed you? I mean, you said the other day that you had no interest in Silas."

"I know, but I wanted to throw them off track." Anna swallowed hard. "I've gotta tell them the truth now; there's no other way."

Rachel rubbed her fingers in little circles across the bridge of her nose. This wasn't good. Not good at all. Anna was lying to Mom and Dad and saying *verhuddelt* things about leaving the Amish faith. How could she be so mixed up? What in the world was happening to their family?

Rachel had every intention of questioning her sister further but Dad stepped onto the porch. "Let's go into the kitchen, Anna." He pointed at Rachel. "You'd better go on up to bed."

Obediently, Rachel stood up, offering Anna a feeble smile. At this rate, she'd never find out the whole story.

When Rachel entered the kitchen, she discovered her mother working on a quilt. A variety of lush greens lay beside vivid red patches spread out on the table like a jigsaw puzzle.

"Ain't it nice?" Mom asked as she glanced up at Rachel. "This is gonna be for Anna's hope chest, seein' as to how she's got herself an interested suitor and all. Why, did you know that she sneaked off yesterday just to be with Silas Swartley? The little scamp told us she wasn't interested in him, but it seems she's changed her mind."

Before Rachel could comment, Dad and Anna entered the room. *"Gut Nacht,* Rachel," Dad said, nodding toward the hallway door.

"Gut Nacht," Rachel mumbled as she exited the room, only closing the door partway. She stopped on the stairwell, out of sight from those in the kitchen. She knew it was wrong to eavesdrop, but she simply couldn't go to bed until she found out what was going on.

"Anna, you said ya had somethin' to say," Dad's voice boomed from the kitchen. "Seems as though ya oughtta start by explainin' why you're so late."

"She was probably with Silas again," Mom interjected. "Anna, we don't have a problem with him courtin' you, but we just can't have ya out after dark. It's much too dangerous."

Rachel knew Anna was taking the time to think before she spoke because there was a long pause. Suddenly, her sister blurted, "I lied about me and Silas. He's not courtin' me, and I'm leavin' the faith!"

Rachel peered through the crack in the doorway and saw Mom's face blanch.

"You're what?" Dad hollered.

"I–I got married today," Anna stammered.

"You were supposed to be at Emma's," Mom said as though the word *married* had never been mentioned.

"What are you talkin' about, Girl?" Dad sputtered.

"Me and Reuben Yutzy got married today by a justice of the peace in Lancaster," Anna announced, her voice sounding stronger by the minute. "We've been seein' each other secretly for some time now, and yesterday we went to get our marriage license."

Rachel's hand flew to her mouth as she stifled a gasp.

"What would cause you to do such a thing?" Dad bellowed. His back was to Rachel, and she could only imagine how red his face must be.

"If it's Reuben ya love and wanted to marry, why'd ya hide it?" Mom questioned. "Why didn't ya speak with the bishop and have him announce in church that ya wanted to be *published?* We could have had the weddin' this fall, and—"

"Reuben and I are leavin' the Amish faith," Anna interrupted.

"You can't be serious about this!" Dad hollered.

"Daniel, you'll wake the whole house," Mom said, sounding close to tears. "Can't we discuss this in a quiet manner?"

Dad cleared his throat and shuffled his feet a few times, the way he always did when he was trying to get himself calmed down. A chair scraped across the kitchen floor. "Sit down, Daughter, and explain this rebellious act of yours."

Rachel stood there, twisting the corners of her apron, too afraid to even breathe. Nothing like this had ever happened in the Beachy home, and she couldn't imagine how it would all turn out.

"Reuben and I have been in love for some time, but we both feel as though the Amish rules ain't right for us no more. We didn't want anyone to know our plans, so I pretended I was seein' Silas yesterday."

Rachel leaned against the wall, feeling as if her whole world was caving in. How could she have been so blind? Anna had been telling her that she didn't love Silas, yet she'd been leading the poor fellow on. She'd been acting secretive and kind of pensive lately, too.

"As you probably know, Reuben's got himself a job workin' for a paint contractor in Lancaster," Anna continued. "That's where we plan to live. I just came home tonight to explain things and gather up my belongings. Reuben's comin' to get me tomorrow mornin'."

"I won't hear this kind of talk in my house!" There was a thud, and Rachel was pretty sure her father's hand had connected with the kitchen table.

"Oh, Daniel, now look what you've gone and done," Mom said tearfully. "All my squares are *verhuddelt*."

"Our daughter's just announced that she's gotten married today and plans to leave the faith, and all you can think about is your mixed-up quiltin' squares? What's wrong with you, *Frau?*"

"But. . .but. . .Anna was raised in the Amish faith," Mom blubbered. "She knows we don't hold to bein' one with the world."

Rachel chanced another peek, just to see how things were looking. Dad was pacing back and forth across the faded linoleum. Mom was gathering up her quilting pieces. Anna was just sitting there with her arms folded across her chest.

"I know ya don't understand, but I've not been happy with our way of life for some time now," Anna asserted.

Dad slapped his hands together, and Rachel jumped back behind the door. "I'll not have ya talkin' thataway! You're our firstborn child, Anna, and it's gonna break your *mamm's* heart if ya run off and leave your faith behind."

"It's not *my* faith I'd be leavin'," Anna said, sounding even more sure of herself. "I'd be turning from my Amish upbringing because it's not somethin' I believe in anymore."

"You were baptized into the church," Mom said softly.

"I know," Anna replied, "but I've come to think the reason I've been feelin' so discontent is because I'm not meant to be one of you. Reuben feels the selfsame way."

"Maybe I should have a little talk with Reuben Yutzy," Dad threatened. "Might could be that he'll come to his senses once I set him straight on a few things."

"You'd have to give up your way of dress if ya left," Mom put in. "You'd be expected to become part of the world. Surely ya must realize the seriousness of all this."

Dad's fist pounded the table again. "You can't do this, Anna. I forbid it!"

Rachel shuddered. Whenever their father forbade anyone in the family to do anything, that was the end of it, plain and simple. No arguments. No discussion. Nothing. The Beachy children had been taught to believe in the Scripture, "Children, obey your parents." Rachel knew that to do anything less meant a sound *bletching* when they were *kinder* and a harsh tongue-lashing, confinement to one's room, or a double dose of chores when they were older. Surely Anna would come to her senses and do what was right.

A muffled sob, followed by, "I'm sorry, Dad, but my mind's made up," told Rachel all she needed to know. Her oldest sister was about to be shunned!

ಶಿ

Morning came much too quickly as far as Rachel was concerned. She awoke feeling like she hadn't slept at all. Part of her heart went out to her sister, for she seemed so sincere in her proclamation about loving Reuben and wanting to leave the Amish faith. Another part of Rachel felt sorry for poor, lovesick Silas. What was he going to say when he got wind of this terrible news? He'd been friends with Anna a long time and had brought her home from a singing not long ago. He must believe he had a chance with her.

And what about the greenhouse? Who would help Mom and Dad with that? Anna had been working there for several years, and the folks sure weren't getting any younger. Eventually they'd need someone to take it over completely.

Rachel slipped out of her nightgown and into a dress, feeling like the weight of the world was resting on her shoulders. She'd be the one asked to fill in for Anna at the greenhouse, she was sure of it. Joseph liked flowers well enough, but he was busy working the fields, and Dad often helped out in the fields—especially during harvest season. If Rachel were forced into the confines of the stuffy, humid greenhouse, she'd hardly have any time for watching birds, hiking, or fishing. She knew it was selfish, but she was more than a little miffed at Anna for sticking her with this added responsibility.

A sudden ray of hope ignited in Rachel's heart. *With Anna leavin', Silas might begin to take notice that I'm alive.* She poured water from the pitcher on her dresser into the washing bowl and smiled. *Guess I could even tolerate workin' with flowers all day if I had a chance at love with Silas.*

Rachel splashed some water on her face, hoping the stinging cold might get her thinking straight. As the cool liquid made contact, she allowed her anxiety to fully surface. Silas wasn't going to turn to her just because Anna was no longer available. Besides, even if by some miracle he did, Rachel would be his second choice. She'd be like yesterday's warmed-over stew.

Her shoulders drooped with anguish and a feeling of hopelessness. She wasn't sure she wanted Silas's love if it had to be that way. But then, she *was* a beggar, and beggars couldn't be choosy.

Rachel hung her nightgown on a wall peg and put her head covering in place. She looked ready enough to face the day, but in her heart she sure wasn't. She hated the thought of going downstairs. After Dad had yelled some more last night, then sent Anna to her room to think things over and pray on it, Rachel had a pretty good notion what things would be like with the start of this new day.

A sudden knock pulled Rachel out of her troubling thoughts. "Rachel, are ya up?" Anna called through the closed door.

"Jah. Just gettin' dressed. Tell Mom I'll be right down to help with breakfast."

"Could I come in? I need to talk."

"Sure, you're more'n welcome."

When Anna opened the door, Rachel could see that she'd been crying. Probably most of the night, truth be told. She also noticed that her sister's hope chest was at her feet.

Anna bent down and pushed the cumbersome trunk into Rachel's room. "I can't stay long," she said in a quavery voice. "I'll be leavin' soon, but I wanted you to have this."

Rachel's heart slammed into her chest. She'd really hoped that after a good night's sleep her stubborn sister might have changed her mind about leaving home. Of course, as far as Anna knew, Rachel hadn't heard what she'd told the folks last night.

"You're leavin'? Where are ya goin'?" Rachel asked, making no mention of the hope chest Anna had slid to the end of her bed.

"Last night after ya went upstairs, I told Mom and Dad that I've been secretly seein' Reuben Yutzy." Anna took a seat on the edge of Rachel's bed. "We got married yesterday," she murmured. "Reuben went home to tell his folks, and I came here to tell ours. Last night was the final time for me to sleep in my old room because this mornin' Reuben's comin' for me and we're leavin' the faith."

Rachel sucked in her breath and flopped down beside her sister. "Leavin' the faith? But where will you go?"

"We'll be livin' in an apartment in Lancaster."

"What'd the folks say about all this, Anna?"

"They're upset, of course. Last night Dad even forbade me to go. Said I had to go up to my room to think and pray on the matter." Anna sniffed. "Guess maybe he hoped I'd see things in a different light come mornin'."

"And do ya?"

Anna shook her head and reached over to pat Rachel's arm. "No, Silly. I love Reuben, and my place is with him."

"What about your hope chest?" Rachel's voice dropped to a near whisper. "Won'tcha be needin' all your things now that you're married and about to set up housekeepin'?"

Anna shook her head. "The apartment Reuben rented is fully furnished. Besides, the things in that chest would only be painful reminders of my past." She nodded at Rachel. "Better that you have 'em."

Rachel was sorely tempted to tell her sister there wasn't much point in her having one hope chest, much less two, since she would probably never marry. She thought better of it, though, because she could see from the look on Anna's face that saying good-bye was hurting her real bad.

"If you renounce your faith, you and Reuben will be shunned. . .probably excommunicated. You've both been baptized into membership, Anna. Have ya forgotten that?"

Anna blew out her breath. "Of course I haven't forgotten.

Leavin' home and family is the sacrifice we're gonna have to make. There ain't no other way."

Rachel jumped up. "Yes, there is! You can forget all this nonsense 'bout becomin' an Englisher. You can stay right here and marry Reuben again, in the Amish church." Strangely enough, Rachel found herself wishing Anna had accepted Silas's offer to court her. With him, at least, she knew Anna would be staying in the faith.

What am I thinkin'? Rachel fretted. *Here I am, so in love with Silas that my heart could burst, and I'm wishin' my sister could be makin' plans to marry him. Maybe I am silly, after all.*

Rachel looked at Anna, and her eyes filled with tears. "What about Silas? You rode home with him in his courtin' buggy from a singin' not long ago. Didn't that mean anything a'tall?"

"I didn't mean to lead Silas on," Anna said sincerely. "I love Reuben, and that's all that matters."

Rachel clenched her fists. It wasn't all that mattered! What about Silas's feelings, and what about their family? Didn't Anna care that her leaving would tear the family apart? How could she be so unfeeling?

"Even if I weren't plannin' to leave, I wouldn't have married Silas," Anna continued. "I don't love him. I never have."

Rachel planted her hands on her hips and looked into Anna's darkened eyes. What had happened to her pleasant childhood playmate? "Silas is a wonderful man, and he loves you. Don't that count for anything?" she shouted.

Anna frowned. "I'm sorry for Silas, but I've gotta go with my heart." She closed her eyes and drew in a deep breath. "What do *you* want out of life, Rachel?"

Rachel swallowed hard. "That's easy. I want love. . .marriage. . .and lots of *kinder.*"

"Since you're so worried over Silas, why don'tcha try to

make him happy? I know ya care for him, so go after Silas. Might could be that the two of you will marry, and he'll give you a whole houseful of *kinder.*"

Rachel hung her head. "I can't make Silas happy. He don't love me."

seven

Not one word was said during breakfast about Anna's plans to leave. It was almost as if nothing had even gone on last night. Rachel figured her folks were hoping Anna's thinking would have righted itself during the night and this morning life would be just as it always had been in the Beachys' home.

When breakfast was over, Dad went outside. Rachel was at the sink doing dishes, and when she glanced out the window, she saw him hitch up the buggy and head down the road. She thought it was odd that he hadn't even said where he was going.

A short time later, Dad returned with Bishop Weaver. Rachel and Elizabeth were out in the garden when she saw the two men climb out of their buggies.

Rachel straightened and pressed a hand against her lower back to ease some of the kinks. The bishop nodded at her. "Where's your sister Anna? I hear tell she's given this family some rather distressin' news."

Before Rachel could reply, Anna came out of the house lugging an old suitcase down the steps.

Bishop Weaver marched over to her and shook his finger right in her face. "I understand you're thinkin' of leavin' the Amish faith."

Rachel dropped the beet she'd just dug up and held her breath. She feared the worst was coming, and there was nothing she could do about it.

"I'm afraid you're a bit confused, Anna," Bishop Weaver said. "Your folks have raised you well, of that much I'm sure."

"Mom and Dad had nothin' to do with my decision to

marry Reuben and leave home," Anna said quickly. "It was my own choice to do so."

The bishop's face flamed, and Rachel felt a sudden need to stand up for her sister. She took a deep breath and walked right over to where they were standing. "I'm sure Anna must have a powerful *gut* reason for wantin' to become English," she boldly proclaimed.

Dad, who'd been standing quietly next to the bishop, finally spoke up. "Rachel Beachy, you had your chance to talk Anna into courtin' Silas, and ya didn't succeed. So, this matter is none of your business!"

Rachel blinked. She guessed it had been a mistake to say anything on Anna's behalf.

"I don't like disappointin' my family," Anna put in, "but I'm a married woman now, and I've gotta be with my husband."

The bishop crossed his arms. "And you're both plannin' to leave the faith?"

Anna nodded.

"Is that your final answer?"

"It has to be."

Bishop Weaver turned toward Dad. "I'm sorry, Daniel. Guess there's nothin' more to be said, unless Anna and Reuben change their minds." With that, he marched back to his buggy.

Anna looked up at her father with tears in her eyes. "Sorry, but I won't be changin' my mind, and I don't think Reuben will neither."

Dad said nothing in return. He stared at Anna a few seconds, like he was looking right through her, then he stalked off.

Rachel didn't know what she could say, either. She felt sick at heart over the way things were going. If Anna left the faith, nothing would ever be the same at home.

A few minutes later, Reuben pulled up in a fancy, red truck. Anna climbed into the passenger's seat, and without even a wave, they were gone.

Rachel felt like breaking down and sobbing, but she didn't. Instead, she got busy and finished up in the garden, then spent the rest of the day helping Mom and Elizabeth can several jars of pickled beets. It kept her hands busy enough, but her mind kept going over the sorrowful events of the last twenty-four hours. Rachel couldn't believe her big sister had actually moved out of the house.

❧

Rachel tossed and turned in her bed that night. Knowing Anna wasn't in her room across the hall left a huge empty spot in Rachel's heart. Even though she was five years younger than her older sister, Rachel and Anna had always been close. They played together when they were small and worked side by side as they grew up. Until recently, they'd shared secrets and similar hopes for their future. Rachel had known Anna was becoming dissatisfied with the Amish way of life, but she hadn't realized how far things had gone. It amazed her that Anna had been able to keep such a secret and not have any of the family suspect anything.

Rachel closed her eyes and tried to picture Anna married to Reuben Yutzy, making their home in Lancaster, wearing English clothes, and living the fancy, modern life. It was all too much to comprehend.

"Does Silas know?" Rachel whispered into the night. *Surely his heart will be broken over this. He's not only lost Anna to the modern world, but to his best friend.* Thinking about Silas helped Rachel feel a little less sorry for herself. She would have to remember to pray for him often.

Ping! Ping! Rachel rolled over in bed. What was that strange noise? *Ping! Ping!* There it was again. She sat up and swung her legs over the side of the bed. It sounded like something was being thrown against her bedroom window.

She hurried across the room and lifted the window's dark shade. In the glow of the moonlight she could see someone standing on the ground below. It was a man, and he was tossing pebbles at her window!

"Who'd be wantin' to get my attention at this time of night?" Rachel muttered as she grabbed her robe off the end of the bed.

Quietly, so she wouldn't wake any of the family, Rachel tiptoed barefoot down the stairs. When she reached the back door, she opened it cautiously and peered out. Bathed in the moonlight, she could see Silas Swartley standing on the grass.

Rachel slipped out the door and ran across the lawn. "Silas, what are ya doin' out here in the dark, throwin' pebbles at my window?"

Silas whirled around to face her. "Rachel?"

She nodded. *"Jah,* it's me. What's up, anyhow?"

Silas shifted his long legs. "I—uh—thought it was Anna's window I was throwin' stones at. I've been wantin' to speak with her but never seem to get the chance."

Rachel's heartbeat quickened. So Silas didn't know. He couldn't have heard the news yet, or else he would have realized Anna wasn't here. She took a few steps closer and impulsively reached out to touch his arm. "Anna's not in her room, Silas."

"She's not? Where is she then?"

Rachel knew her lower lip quivered, but she seemed powerless to stop it. She pressed her lips tightly together, trying to compose herself. This was going to be a lot harder than she'd thought. "I hate to be the one tellin' ya this," she began slowly, "but Anna ran off and got married last night. She left home this mornin'."

Silas's mouth dropped open like a window with a broken hinge. "Married? Left home?" He stared off into space as though he were in a daze, and Rachel's heart went out to him. She had to tell Silas the rest. He had the right to know. Besides, if he didn't hear it from her, he was bound to find out sooner or later. News like this traveled fast, especially when an Amish church member left the faith to become English.

"Anna married Reuben Yutzy. They're leavin' the church, and—"

"Reuben? My *gut* friend?"

Rachel nodded. The motion was all she could manage, given the circumstances. Even in the darkness she could see the pained expression on Silas's face.

"This can't be. It just can't be," he muttered.

Rachel swallowed against the lump in her throat. If only she could take away his pain. If she could just think of a way to make her sister come home. *But what good would that do? Anna's already married to Reuben and nothin' is gonna change that fact.*

Silas began to pace. "I knew Reuben was dissatisfied with our way of life. I also knew he was hangin' around some English fellows who were leadin' him astray." He stopped, turned, and slowly shook his head. "I just had no idea Anna was in on it."

Rachel felt herself tremble. She didn't know if her shivering was from the cool grass tickling her bare feet or if it stemmed from the anger she felt rising in her soul. There was only one thing she was certain of—Silas was trying to lay part of the blame on her sister's shoulders.

"Listen here," she said with a tremor in her voice, "Anna wasn't *in* on this. She became *part* of it because she loves Reuben and wanted to be with him."

"Did she tell you that?"

"Not in so many words, but she did say she and Reuben have been secretly seein' each other and that they're in love."

Silas snorted. "She probably influenced him to make the break. Anna always has been a bit of a rebel."

Rachel's heart was thumping so hard she feared it might burst. How dare Silas speak of her sister that way! She gasped for breath, grateful for the cool night air to help clear her head.

"Anna might have a mind of her own," she snapped, "but she's not the kind of person who would try to sway someone else to leave the church. I have a pretty good notion Reuben wanted to go English as much as Anna did. Maybe even more."

୨ଈ

Silas drew in a deep breath, trying to get control of his emotions. It seemed like his whole world was falling apart, but he knew he had no right to blame Anna for everything. He'd just talked to Reuben a few days ago, and his friend had made it clear that he wanted many of the things the world had to offer. He was working for an English man, was running around with the English doing all sorts of worldly things, and Reuben had even told Silas he wasn't happy being Amish anymore. Truth be told, Silas had been expecting Reuben to leave the faith. What he hadn't expected was that Anna Beachy would be leaving, too—especially not as Reuben Yutzy's wife!

"If I could make things different, I would," Rachel said, breaking into Silas's troubling thoughts. He looked down at her and noticed that her chin was quivering. For one brief moment, Silas was tempted to take Rachel into his arms and offer comforting words. Trouble was, he had no words of comfort. . .for Rachel or himself. All he was feeling was anger and betrayal. His best friend had taken his girl, and Anna had led him on all these years. How could he ever come to grips with that knowledge?

Silas dipped his head in apology. "Sorry for snappin' at ya, Rachel. I know none of this is your fault. It's just such a shock to find out you've lost not one, but two special friends in the same day." He sniffed. "This had to be goin' on between Reuben and Anna for some time, and I was too blind to see it. What a dunce I've been, thinkin' Anna and I had a future together. Why, I chased after her like a horse runnin' toward a bucket of fresh oats, even though she kept pushin' me away. She must have thought I was *Ab im Kopp*."

Rachel grabbed his arm and gave it a good shake. "Stop talkin' thataway! You're not off in the head for lovin' someone. Reuben had you fooled, and Anna had our whole family fooled." She shook her head. "No one's to blame but Anna and Reuben. They should've been honest with everyone involved. They shouldn't have waited so long to tell us their plans."

Silas nodded. "You're right, Rachel. They deserve to be shunned."

Rachel grimaced. "That's the part I dislike the most. It's hard enough to have Anna leave home, knowin' she'll be livin' as one with the world. To realize we have to shun our own kin is the worst part of all."

Silas blew out his breath. "*Jah,* but we have no other choice. It's the old way of doin' things, and it will most likely always be so." He took a few steps backward. "Guess I should be gettin' on home. My mission here is over. As much as it pains me to say it, Anna's outta my life for good."

Rachel rubbed her hands briskly over her arms, like she might be getting cold, and for the second time tonight, Silas was tempted to embrace her. He caught himself in time, remembering Anna's words the other day when she'd said she thought Rachel might be interested in him. If he hugged her, even in condolence, she might get the wrong idea. No, it would be better if he didn't say or do anything to lead young Rachel on. Things were messed up enough. No sense making one more mistake.

"See ya at the next preachin'," Silas said before he turned and sprinted up the driveway, where his horse and buggy stood waiting. Rachel Beachy would have to find comfort from her family, and he would find solace through his work on the farm.

eight

It was the first day of August, and an unreal stillness hung in the hot, sticky air. It was like an oven inside the house, so Rachel wandered outside after lunch, hoping to find a cool breeze. She found, instead, her younger brother and sister, engaged in an all-out water skirmish.

Squeals of laughter permeated the air as the twins ran back and forth to the water trough, filling their buckets and flinging water on one another until they were both drenched from head to toe.

Rachel chuckled at their antics and stepped off the porch, thinking she might join them. The flash of a colorful wing caught her attention instead. Her gaze followed the flitting bird to a nearby willow tree. Like a magnet, she followed the goldfinch as it sailed from tree to tree, finally stopping at one of the feeders in the flower garden. When it had eaten its fill, it flew over to the birdbath. Dipping its tiny black head up and down, the finch drank of the fresh water Rachel had put there early that morning.

Rachel loved watching the birds that came into their yard. Loved hearing their melodic songs. Loved everything about nature.

Per-chick-o-ree, the finch called.

"Per-chick-o-ree," Rachel echoed.

She watched until the bird flew out of sight, then she moved across the yard toward the clothesline. In this heat, she knew the clothes she'd washed and hung this morning would definitely be dry.

Rachel heard a small voice, and she looked down. Apparently

Elizabeth had given up her water battle with Perry, for she was crouched next to the basket of clothes. Her usually pinned-up braids hung down the back of her sopping wet dress like two limp rags. "Dad says Anna will come to her senses and return home again. What do you think, Rachel?" the child asked.

Rachel knelt next to her sister and wrapped her arms around the little girl's small shoulders. "We're all hopin' Anna will return to us, but it might never happen."

"How come?"

"Anna has it in her mind that she wants to live as the English do. I hear tell she's workin' as a waitress at a restaurant in Lancaster. She and Reuben are married now, and they've settled into an apartment there."

"Why can't they live here with us?" Elizabeth asked, her blue eyes looking ever so serious.

Rachel drew in a deep breath. How was she going to explain something to her little sister that she didn't understand herself? "Well," she began, "Reuben and Anna don't think our ways are so good anymore."

"Why not?"

"It's like this—"

"Rachel Beachy, what do ya think you're doin', fillin' Elizabeth's head with such talk?" Dad's deep voice cut through the air like a knife, cutting Rachel off in midsentence. He grabbed Elizabeth's arm and pulled her to her feet. "Get on up to the house and change outta those wet clothes. Your *mamm's* been lookin' for ya, and I'm sure she's got somethin' useful you can be doin'."

As soon as Elizabeth was gone, Dad turned to face Rachel. "You oughta be ashamed, talkin' to Elizabeth like that. She's young and don't understand things of the world just yet. She might think what Anna's done is perfectly okay."

"Elizabeth meant no harm in askin', and I didn't think it

would hurt to try to explain things a bit." Rachel's eyes filled with unwanted tears, and she bit her lip, hoping to keep them at bay. Things were bad enough around here; she sure didn't want any hard feelings between her and Dad.

"Jah, well, be careful what you say from now on," Dad said, his voice softening some. "We've lost one daughter to the world, and I sure don't want any of my other *kinder* gettin' such crazy thoughts." He turned toward the greenhouse, calling over his shoulder, "When you're done with the laundry, I could use your help. We're likely to have lots more customers today!"

Rachel grabbed another towel from the wicker basket and gave it a good snap. *"Immer Druwel ergitz*—always trouble somewhere," she mumbled.

❧

It was another warm day, and Rachel, accompanied by Elizabeth, had gone into town to buy some things their mother was needing. Since Dad paid Rachel a little something for working in the greenhouse, she bought a few new things for her hope chest—just in case.

"How 'bout some lunch?" Rachel asked her sister when they finished shopping. "Are ya hungry?"

Elizabeth giggled and scrambled quickly into the buggy. "You know me, Rachel. . .I'm always hungry."

"Where would ya like to go?" Rachel asked, tucking her packages behind the seat, then taking up the reins.

"I don't care. Why don't you choose?"

Rachel nodded and steered the horse in the direction of the Good 'n Plenty, a family-style restaurant located on the other side of town.

The restaurant was crowded with summer tourists, and the girls had to wait to be seated. Elizabeth needed to use the rest room, so Rachel waited for her in the hallway outside the door. A man walked by wearing a baseball cap with an inscription on the front that read "Born to Fish. Forced to Work!"

Yep, that's me, Rachel thought ruefully. *I'd love to go fishin' every day and never have to work in the greenhouse again.*

As the fisherman disappeared, Rachel caught a glimpse of an Amish man coming from the kitchen, but she thought nothing of it until she got a good look at him. It was Silas Swartley, and he was heading her way.

"It's good to see you, Rachel. How are things?"

Rachel swiped her tongue across her parched lips. Except for biweekly preaching services, she hadn't seen much of Silas since that night he'd come to the house looking for Anna. The fact that she'd been the one to give him the shocking news about her sister running off with his best friend still stuck in Rachel's craw. It should have been Reuben or Anna doing the telling. But no, they left without thinking of anyone but themselves. Seeing Silas standing here now, looking so handsome, yet unapproachable, gave Rachel a funny feeling way down deep inside.

Silas was holding a wooden crate in his hands. "Well, has the cat got your tongue, or are ya gonna answer my question?" he teased.

"W—what question was that?"

"I asked how things are."

"About the same as usual, I guess," she replied with a slight nod. "How's it at your place?"

"Everything's about the same with us, too," he said with a silly grin. "I brought in a crate of fresh potatoes from our farm. This restaurant buys a lot of produce from us." Silas tipped his head toward Rachel. "How come you're here?"

"Elizabeth and I came to town for a few things. We're here for lunch." She suppressed a giggle. "Why else would we be at the Good 'n Plenty?"

Silas's tanned face turned red like a cherry tomato, and he stared down at his black work boots. "I don't suppose you've heard anything from Anna."

Rachel swallowed against the nodule that had lodged in her throat. Of course Silas would ask about Anna. He was still in love with her. Truth be told, Silas was probably hoping Anna would give up her silly notion about being English and come back to the valley again. But then, even if she did, what good would that do him? Anna was a married woman now—out-of-bounds for Silas Swartley.

"Anna's made no direct contact with us," Rachel said flatly. "She did send Martha Rose a letter, though."

Silas looked a bit hopeful. "What'd it say?"

"Just that she and Reuben are settled now. She got herself a job as a waitress, and Reuben's still paintin' houses and all." Rachel's nose twitched. "Guess they've gotta have lots of money, since they're livin' in the modern world and will probably be buyin' all sorts of fancy gadgets."

Silas's dark eyebrows furrowed. "*Jah,* I reckon so. Sure wish Anna would've waited a while to marry Reuben and not run off like that. Maybe if she'd given it more thought and given me more time, I coulda won her heart."

Rachel shrugged. "She's gone now, and I'm pretty sure she's never comin' back."

Silas squinted his dark eyes. "How do ya know that?"

"I just do, that's all. My sister's walkin' a different path now, and she made it real clear that it was her choice."

Silas shook his head. "I've known Anna since we were *kinder,* and I always thought we were *gut* friends. It's awful hard to accept the idea that there's no future for me and her."

Rachel's heart ached for Silas, but more than that, it ached for herself. She was sure he would always love Anna, even if they couldn't be together. So much for hoping he might ever be interested in plain little Rachel. Hopeless, useless daydreams would get her nowhere, yet no matter how hard she tried to push it aside, the dream remained. "The future rests in God's hands," she mumbled, turning away.

&

Silas left the Good 'n Plenty feeling like someone had punched him in the stomach. Anna wasn't coming home. Rachel had confirmed his worst fears. Old memories tugged at his heart. He'd trusted Anna, and she had betrayed that trust. Could he ever trust another woman? *Even if she does change her mind and come back, she'll never be mine,* he thought ruefully. *She's a married woman now. . .married to my best friend!*

Deep in his heart, Silas knew he had to accept things as they were and get on with life, but no matter how hard he tried, he just couldn't imagine any kind of life without Anna Beachy.

Poor Rachel—she looked so sad. Anna's leavin' must have hurt her nearly as much as it did me. He would have to remember to pray for her and all the Beachys. No Amish family ever really got over one of their own running off to become English, and from the look on Rachel's face, he figured she had a long ways to go in overcoming her grief.

&

"Was that Silas Swartley you were talkin' to?" Elizabeth asked when she stepped out of the ladies' room.

Rachel nodded. "It was him."

Elizabeth looked up at her expectantly, like she thought Rachel should say something more.

Rachel merely shrugged. "He was askin' about Anna."

"He was real sweet on her, ain't it so?"

"Jah, he was. I'm afraid he is very much broken up over her leavin'."

Elizabeth grabbed Rachel's hand and gave it a squeeze. "Anna's never comin' back, is she?"

"Probably not, unless it's just for a visit."

"Could we go to Lancaster sometime? I'd surely like to see my big sister again."

"That wouldn't be a *gut* idea," Rachel said, pulling her sister along as they made their way down the hall.

"Why not?" the child persisted. "I miss Anna a lot."

Rachel felt sick at heart for she missed her older sister, too. How could she explain it to Elizabeth when she couldn't make sense of it herself? If they went to Lancaster to see Anna, Dad would be furious. Not only that, but Elizabeth might like the modern way Anna was living and decide to seek after worldly things herself. No, it would be better for all if they never paid a visit to Anna.

"Your table is ready now," a young Mennonite waitress said as they approached the dining room.

Rachel smiled, glad for the diversion. Maybe after they were seated, Elizabeth's mind would be on her empty stomach and not on Anna. Might could be that the discussion would be dropped altogether and they could eat a quiet, peaceful lunch.

Much to Rachel's chagrin, no sooner had they placed their orders, when the questions began again.

"Are Mom and Dad mad at Anna?" Elizabeth blinked several times. "They never talk about her anymore."

Rachel drew in a deep breath and offered up a silent prayer. She needed God's wisdom just now, for sure as anything she didn't want to make things worse by telling her sensitive, young sister something that might upset her even more. "It's like this," she began, carefully choosing her words, "Mom and Dad love Anna very much, but they also love bein' Amish. They believe in the *Ordnung* and want to abide by the rules of our church."

Elizabeth nodded soberly. "I've tried talkin' about Anna several times, but Dad always says it would be best if I'd just forget I ever had an older sister. How can I do that, Rachel? Anna's still my big sister, ain't it so?"

Rachel reached across the table and gently touched Elizabeth's small hand. "Of course she's your sister. Nothin' will ever change that." She sighed deeply. "The thing is, Anna's moved away now, and she's wantin' to live like the English."

Elizabeth's lower lip trembled. "She really don't wanna be Amish no more?"

"I'm afraid not. But we can surely pray that someday she and Reuben will change their minds and be willin' to reconcile with the church through repenting and confession before the bishop and the congregation." Rachel was grateful that their district's rules for shunning weren't as strict as some, where absolutely all contact with banned church members was forbidden. Bishop Weaver had made it clear that, as outcasts, Reuben and Anna should be avoided, although limited contact with them would be allowed. But he was firm in stating that church members were not to do any business with them or eat at the same table with them unless they repented and returned to the faith.

Rachel felt hot tears stinging the backs of her eyes. Today had started off well enough, but after seeing Silas and talking about Anna with him and now trying to make Elizabeth understand, she felt all done in. She had no answers. Not for Silas, not for Elizabeth, and not for herself. As far as Rachel was concerned, life would never be the same. She lifted her water glass and took a sip. If only there was some way she could get Silas to notice her now that Anna was out of his life. If only God would make Silas love her and not Anna.

As she set the glass back down, a little voice in Rachel's head reminded her that God never forced a person to love anyone—not even Him. If Silas was ever going to get over losing Anna, it would have to be because *he* chose to do so.

I can still hope, Rachel mused. *The Bible says in Psalm 71:14, "But I will hope continually and will yet praise thee more and more."*

nine

The Beachys were all sitting on the front porch because it was still too hot inside to go to bed. Mom was in her wheelchair, mending one of Joseph's shirts. Dad sat beside her in the rocker, reading the Amish newspaper called *The Budget*. Joseph and Perry were sitting on the steps, playing a game, and Rachel shared the porch swing with Elizabeth. It was a quiet, peaceful night, in spite of the sweltering August heat.

Rachel mechanically pumped her legs as she gazed out at the fireflies rising from the grass. An owl hooted from a nearby tree and the sun dipped slowly below the horizon, transforming the sky into a hazy pink. If not for the fact that she still missed Anna so much and had been forced to take her place in the greenhouse several hours a day, Rachel would have felt a sense of contentment as she soaked up the aura of beauty God's hand had provided.

Of course, I've lost Silas, too, she reminded herself. Ever since Anna and Reuben left, Rachel sensed that Silas was mourning his loss. She'd seen him at preaching services several times, and no matter how hard she tried to be friendly, he remained aloof. *Maybe I should give up the hope of him ever seein' me as a woman he could love.* "It's all just a silly dream," she murmured.

"What'd ya say?" Elizabeth asked, nudging Rachel with her elbow.

Rachel felt her face flush. "Nothin'. I was just thinkin' out loud."

"Daydreamin' is probably more like it," Joseph said with a chuckle. "I've never known anyone who could stare off into space the way you do and see nothin' a'tall. A daydreamin' little tomboy, that's our Rachel."

Rachel grimaced. Was Joseph looking for an argument tonight? Maybe he'd had a rough day out in the fields. Could be that Perry had been goofing around and didn't help much. Or the hot weather might be making her big brother a bit cross.

"If ya ever plan on any man marryin' you, then you'd better turn in your fishin' pole for a broom," Joseph continued. "A grown woman ain't supposed to climb trees, wade in the river, and stand around for hours gawkin' at dumb birds."

Rachel folded her arms across her chest and squinted at Joseph. "I refuse to let you ruffle my feathers."

He snickered. "Aw, I wasn't tryin' to upset ya. I was just funnin', that's all."

Rachel shrugged. "I thought maybe you were *gridlich* 'cause ya had a rough day."

"I think we're all a bit cranky," Dad spoke up. "A few more swelterin' days like this and everything in the garden will dry up, like as not."

Mom nodded. *"Jah,* I've had to water things in the greenhouse a lot more'n usual, too."

"Everyone has their share of troubles," Perry added. "Did ya hear 'bout Katie Swartley breakin' her arm?"

Rachel's ears perked right up. "Silas's *mamm?"*

Perry nodded. "Yep, I heard it from her son Sam this mornin' when we went fishin' in the pond near Swartleys' place."

"When did this happen?" Mom questioned. "And how?"

"Sometime yesterday," Perry answered. "Sam said she fell down the stairs."

Mom clicked her tongue. *"Ach,* poor Katie. How's she gonna manage with only one good arm?"

"Guess her boys will have to chip in and help out more," Dad commented. "It's a downright shame she don't have no girls."

"I could give her a hand," Rachel volunteered, trying to keep her excitement out of her voice. She did feel bad about Katie's arm, but if she could go over there every day, it would give her a chance to see Silas.

"That's a nice thought, Rachel," Dad said, "but you're needed here, especially in the greenhouse. August is a busy time, what with so many tourists comin' by and all. I'm helpin' Joseph and Perry in the fields part of each day, and we sure can't expect your *mamm* to handle things in the greenhouse all by herself."

"How 'bout me?" Elizabeth chimed in. "I like flowers. Can't I help in the greenhouse?"

Mom looked over at Elizabeth and smiled. "I appreciate the offer, but I need someone at the house to get the noon meal fixed."

Joseph turned to face his mother. "Say, I've got an idea."

"And what might that be?" she asked.

"Why don't ya ask Pauline Hostetler to help out with the greenhouse? I know for a fact that she loves flowers."

"And how would ya be knowin' that?" Dad asked, giving Joseph a quick wink.

His face turned beet red and he started squirming a bit.

"Joseph's sweet on Pauline," Perry interjected. "I seen him talkin' to her at the last preachin' service."

Rachel couldn't believe her bashful brother had finally taken the initiative with Pauline. She thought this bit of news might be beneficial to her as well. She jumped off the swing and raced over to her mother's wheelchair. "I really would like to help out at the Swartleys'," she said sincerely. "If Pauline agrees to work at the greenhouse, I'd even be willin' to pay her with some of the money I've already made this summer."

Mom's brows drew together. "Now why would ya do somethin' like that? It's your *daed* and I who should be payin' any hired help, not you, for goodness' sake."

Rachel giggled nervously. If she weren't careful, she'd be giving away her plans to win Silas. "I–I just thought, since you'd have to pay someone to take my place, I'd be obliged to help with their wages."

Mom smiled. "That's very generous of you, Daughter, but it surely won't be necessary."

"I can help Katie Swartley?"

"If it's okay with your *daed,* then it's fine by me," Mom said with a nod.

"Won't bother me none, as long as Pauline agrees to the terms," Dad stated. He looked over at Joseph, who seemed to be studying the checkerboard real hard. "Son, since this was your idea, how 'bout you drivin' over to the Hostetlers' place tomorrow mornin' and askin' Pauline if she'd like to work in the greenhouse for a few weeks?"

Joseph smiled from ear to ear. "Sure, I can do that."

Rachel smiled, too. If things went well, by tomorrow afternoon she might be on her way to winning Silas Swartley's heart.

ぃ

Silas and his younger brothers, Jake, age seventeen, and Sam, who was twelve, had just returned from the fields. Silas spotted a horse and buggy parked in the driveway, but before he could say anything, Jake hollered, "Looks like we've got company!"

"Probably one of Mom's friends come to see if she needs any help," Silas replied with a shrug.

"I hope they brought somethin' good to eat," Sam put in. "Now that Mom's arm is busted, she sure won't be doin' much bakin'."

Silas flicked his little brother's straw hat off his head. "It's the same old story with you, Boy. Always hungry, ain't ya?"

Sam flashed him a freckle-faced grin and bounded up the porch steps. "Last one to the table is a fat cow!"

Silas and his brothers raced into the kitchen, laughing and grabbing at each other's shirts, hoping to be the first ones washed up and seated on their bench at the table.

Jake and Sam were already at the sink, pumping water and lathering up their hands, but Silas stopped short just inside the door. His gaze was fixed on Rachel Beachy, who was busy setting the table. She glanced over at him and smiled, and his heart seemed to stop beating for a few seconds. He'd never noticed it, but Rachel had two little dimples—one in each cheek. Had she never smiled at him before, or had he just been too busy to notice? Today she almost looked like a mature woman. Could she have changed that much since he'd last seen her?

"Guess that's your buggy outside," Silas said, feeling kind of nervous all of a sudden.

"Jah, it's mine, all right," she answered. "I'm here to help your *mamm* 'til her arm gets better."

Silas's mouth dropped open. "You're gonna stay with us?"

"No, Silly. Rachel will be comin' over every mornin' and stayin' until after supper," Mom said.

Silas really felt stupid. Here his mother was standing at the stove, stirring a pot of soup with her one good arm, and he hadn't even noticed her until she spoke up.

He swallowed hard, removed his hat, and hung it on a wall peg. "That's right nice of you, Rachel. Nice of your folks to let you come, too."

Rachel placed a loaf of bread on the table. "If Pauline Hostetler hadn't been willin' to take my place at the greenhouse, I probably couldn't have come."

"Did ya bring anything *gut* to eat?" This question came from young Sam, who had already taken his place at the table.

"Samuel, where are your manners? Sometimes I don't know what gets into my boys," Mom scolded. "Rachel came to help, not furnish the likes of you with all kinds of fattenin' goodies."

Rachel smiled at Sam. "Actually, I did bring some chocolate chip cookies." She motioned toward a basket on the cupboard.

Sam started to get up, but Silas placed a restraining hand on his shoulder. "You'd better eat lunch first, don'tcha think?"

"What is for lunch, and where's Pap?" Jake asked as he joined his brothers at the table.

"Vegetable soup and ham sandwiches, and he's not back from town yet," Mom answered.

Silas and his brothers waited until Rachel and Mom took their seats, then all heads bowed in silent prayer. A short time later everyone had eaten their fill, and Rachel offered the cookies as dessert.

Silas smacked his lips after the first bite. "Umm. . .these are right tasty. You didn't bake 'em yourself, did ya, Rachel?" He laughed, but she didn't.

"Of course," Rachel replied a bit stiffly. "I may be just a little tomboy in some folks' eyes, but I can cook, bake, sew, clean, and do most everything else around the house."

Silas didn't have a clue what he'd said to make Rachel go all peevish on him, but for some reason, she seemed kind of miffed. He shrugged and reached for another cookie. *She sure don't look like no* Hausfrau *to me.*

ॐ

As Rachel cleared away the dishes, her mind was on Silas, who'd gone back out to the fields with his brothers. She sure wished she could figure him out. One minute he was smiling and saying how nice it was for her to help out, and the next minute he was making fun of her.

Was Silas really making fun? a little voice niggled at the back of her mind. *He did say your cookies were good, and he only asked if you'd baked them.* Maybe she was overly sensitive where Silas was concerned. Might could be that she had tried too hard to make him take notice of her by smiling real sweet and bringing those cookies. Maybe she should play hard to get, like some of the other young Amish women often did when they were trying to get a man's attention.

"No, that wouldn't be right," Rachel mumbled as she placed the dirty dishes in the sink. Besides, she was not Anna, so if Silas was going to take notice, then it wouldn't be because she was playing hard to get.

"Did you say somethin'?" Katie asked, drawing Rachel out of her musings.

"I was talkin' to myself," Rachel admitted. She grinned at Katie, whose plump face always seemed to be wearing a smile.

"If you ever need someone to talk to, I've got *gut* ears for lis-tenin'," the older woman said as she wiped down the tablecloth.

Rachel smiled. "I'll remember that." She moved over to the stove to retrieve the pot of water she'd heated to wash the dishes. "I can finish up in here. I'm sure you've gotta be tired by now. Why don'tcha go rest awhile?"

Katie handed Rachel the dishrag. "I think I'll take ya up on that offer. My arm's kinda hurtin', so some aspirin and a good nap might do me some good."

"What else are ya needin' done today?" Rachel asked.

"Let's see now. . .it's too hot to do any bakin', but if you're feelin' like it, maybe you could mix up a ribbon salad." Katie waved her good hand toward the pantry. "I think there's a few packages of gelatin, some walnuts, a can of crushed pineapple, and a bag of marshmallows in there. Last time I checked the refrigerator, we had plenty of whipping cream, milk, and cream cheese, so you should be able to put it together in time for supper."

A short time later, Rachel had prepared the ribbon salad and was just placing it inside the refrigerator, when the back door swung open. Thinking it was probably Herman Swartley returning from town, Rachel turned toward the door and smiled. Her smile was quickly replaced with a frown when she saw Silas standing there, holding his hand

and grimacing in obvious pain.

She hurried to his side, feeling as if her breath had been snatched away. "What is it? Are ya hurt?" Her frown faded to surprise when she heard Silas's answer.

"I got a big old splinter in my thumb, and it's all your fault."

Rachel's hands went straight to her hips. "My fault? How can gettin' a splinter be my fault?"

Silas hung his head, kind of sheepish-like. "I took a handful of your cookies out to the fields, and after I ate a few, I forgot to put my gloves back on. Next thing I knew, I was grabbin' hold of the wagon, and here's what I've got to show for it!" He held up his thumb for her inspection.

Rachel bit back a smile, even though her stomach did a little flip-flop just thinking about how much the sliver must hurt. "So, it's my fault ya weren't wearin' your gloves, huh?"

He nodded and looked her right in the eye, which made her stomach take another nosedive. "If you weren't so *gut* at makin' cookies, I wouldn't have grabbed a handful. And if I'd had my gloves on, I sure wouldn't have all this pain."

Silas's voice had a soft quality about it, yet he spoke with assurance. Rachel thought she could sit and listen to him talk for hours on end. "Take a seat at the table and I'll have a look-see," she instructed, pulling her wayward thoughts back to the need at hand. "Do you know where your *mamm* keeps her needles and such?"

Silas's eyes were wide, and his mouth hung open just a bit. "You're not plannin' to go pokin' around on my thumb, are ya?"

She tipped her head to one side. "Now, how else did ya expect me to remove that old splinter?"

Silas swallowed hard. "Guess you've got a point." He nodded toward the old treadle sewing machine positioned along the wall nearest the stone fireplace. "I think you'll find all your doctorin' tools over there."

Rachel went immediately to the sewing machine and opened the top drawer of the wooden cabinet. Sure enough, there were plenty of needles, a pair of tweezers, and even a magnifying glass. Katie Swartley must have had some experience taking out slivers, her having three boys, a husband, and all.

"It might be best if you close your eyes," Rachel said as she leaned close to Silas and took his big hand in hers. This was the closest she'd ever been to him, and it took all her willpower and concentration to focus on that nasty sliver and not his masculine scent or the feel of his warm breath blowing softly against her face.

"I ain't no *buppli*," Silas said between clenched teeth. "So, I'll keep my eyes open, thank you very much."

"As you like," Rachel replied. She jabbed the needle underneath the sliver and pushed upward.

"Yow! That hurts like crazy!" Silas's face was white as a sheet, and Rachel feared he might be about to pass out.

Rachel clenched her teeth to keep from laughing out loud. So Silas didn't think he was a baby, huh? "Hang your head between your knees and take some deep breaths," she ordered.

As soon as Silas had his head down, Rachel grabbed his hand again and set to work. It was hard to ignore his groans and yowls, but in short order she had the splinter out. "Let me pour some peroxide over it and give you a bandage," she said. "Do you know where those are kept?"

Silas sat up and took several deep breaths before he answered. "In the cupboard, just above the sink."

Soon the wound was cleansed and a bandage was securely in place. Silas smiled at Rachel, and she thought her heart had stopped beating. *How could Anna have turned Silas away in exchange for the likes of Reuben Yutzy, who is doin' all that worldly stuff?*

"*Danki*, Rachel," Silas said, offering her a crooked grin.

"That splinter was a nasty one, and I don't rightly think I coulda taken it out myself."

She licked her lips and smiled back at him. "You're welcome."

Silas stood up and started for the door, but suddenly he pivoted back around. "Say, I was wonderin'. . .that is. . ."

"What were you wonderin'?"

He shook his head and turned toward the door. "Never mind. It weren't nothin' important."

The door clicked behind him and Rachel sank into a chair. Was there any hope for her and Silas, or had she just imagined that he'd looked at her with interest?

ten

Over the next few weeks, Rachel helped Katie nearly every day but Sunday. She would get up an hour early in order to get her own chores done at home, then right after breakfast she'd head over to the Swartleys'. Katie's arm was hurting less, but she would have to wear the cast for another three weeks, which meant she still had the use of only one arm.

Things weren't going as well with Silas as Rachel had hoped. Ever since the day she'd removed his splinter, Silas had seemed kind of distant. She had to wonder if he was trying to avoid her, although she couldn't think why, since she'd made every effort to be pleasant. It might be that Silas's aloofness was just because he was so busy in the fields. On most days, she only saw him during lunch and supper, and even then he appeared tired and withdrawn.

Today was Saturday, and Katie Swartley had enlisted the help of some neighboring Amish women so Rachel could work in the greenhouse with Pauline. Dad had taken Mom, Elizabeth, and Perry to Bird-in-Hand, where they would be selling some of their plants and fresh-cut flowers at the Farmers' Market. Since Saturday was always a big day at the greenhouse, they didn't want to leave Pauline alone to deal with the tourists, who would no doubt be stopping by. Joseph was also left behind to finish up some chores in the barn.

As Rachel began watering plants, the musty scent of wet soil assaulted her senses, causing her to sneeze and making her wish she could be outside instead of cooped up inside a much too warm greenhouse. She glanced over at Pauline, who was waiting on some English customers. The tall, blond-haired woman certainly had changed of late. Instead of being distant and sometimes cross, Pauline had become outgoing and cheerful. Rachel could remember a few years ago, back when Pauline had been jilted by Eli Yoder, she hadn't even tried to hide her bitter feelings. Every chance Pauline got, she told tales about the woman who had stolen Eli's heart. Rachel had often been tempted to tell Pauline that she'd better keep her own garden free of weeds instead of worrying over someone else's, but she never said anything. Pauline was six years older than her and probably wouldn't have listened to any advice from a *kinder.*

Rachel couldn't be sure what had brought about such a dramatic change in Pauline, but she suspected it had something to do with working in the greenhouse. *Of course, my brother Joseph might have had a little influence on her attitude.* Joseph seemed to have set his reservations aside about his and Pauline's age difference. Rachel noticed the way he hung around Pauline every chance he got. Pauline would have to be blind and just plain dumb not to be flattered by all his attention.

When the customers exited the greenhouse, Rachel moved over to the counter. "You can take your lunch break now if ya want. I'll wait on anyone who might come by during the next hour."

Pauline nodded and grabbed her lunch basket from underneath the counter. "Think I'll eat outside. Might as well enjoy the *gut* weather while it lasts. Fall's almost upon us, can ya tell?"

"*Jah.* Mornin' and evenin' seem much cooler now. Won't be no time a'tall 'til the leaves start to change," Rachel remarked.

Pauline was just about to open the door when Rachel called out, "I think Joseph's still in the barn. Would ya mind goin' there and lettin' him know I made a sandwich for him and it's in the refrigerator?"

Pauline smiled. "I think I can do better than that. I'll go on up to the house, fetch the sandwich and somethin' cold to drink, then take it out to Joe myself."

Ah, so it's "Joe," now, is it? Rachel hid her smile behind the writing tablet she'd just picked up. "See you later, Pauline. Tell *Joe* I said hello, and I hope he enjoys his lunch."

The door clicked shut and Rachel moved over to the window and watched Pauline walk down the path toward their house. "I wonder if I should give Anna's old hope chest to her." She shrugged. "Guess maybe I should hang on to it. . . just in case Anna changes her mind and returns home for some of her things."

❧

Silas wasn't sure it was such a good idea to be going to the greenhouse Rachel's mother had named Grandma's Place, but his buggy was already pulling into the graveled parking lot, so he figured he may as well carry out his plans.

When he entered the greenhouse, Rachel greeted Silas from behind the front counter, where she sat reading a book.

"I thought you'd be swamped with customers," he said, removing his straw hat and offering her a smile.

Rachel jumped off her stool and moved swiftly to the other side of the counter. "We were busy earlier, but I think everyone must be eatin' their lunch about now." She took a few steps toward Silas. "I'm surprised to see ya here today."

He shuffled his feet a few times and glanced around the room. "Uh, where's Pauline? I thought she was workin' here now."

Rachel nodded curtly, and her eyebrows drew together.

Have I said somethin' wrong? Silas wondered.

"Pauline does work here, but she's on her lunch break right now. Want me to see if I can find her?" Rachel asked, moving toward the door.

Silas stopped her by placing his hand on her arm. *"Himmel—* no, no. I didn't come by to see Pauline."

"You didn't?"

He shook his head.

"What did ya come for?"

He rocked back and forth on his heels, with one hand balled into a fist and the other one hanging on to his hat real tight. "I—um—was wonderin'. . . That is—"

"Are ya needin' a plant or some cut flowers?" Rachel interrupted. "Mom and Dad took quite a few to the market this mornin', but I think there's still a good supply in the back room."

Silas cleared his throat a few times, trying to decide the best way to broach the subject that had brought him here in the first place. *It sure is gettin' mighty warm.* He fanned his face with his hat, hoping the action might give him something to do with his hands, as well as get him cooled down some.

"You okay, Silas?" Rachel asked with a note of concern. "You're lookin' kinda poorly. Wanna sit down awhile?"

"Jah, maybe that would be a *gut* idea," he said, pulling up an empty crate and plunking down with a groan. "Whew! Don't know what came over me, but I was feelin' a little woozy for a minute."

"Maybe you're comin' down with the flu or somethin'," Rachel said, placing her hand against his forehead. Her fingers felt cool and soft, making it even harder for Silas to think straight.

"I'm not sick," he asserted. "It's just warm in here, that's all."

Rachel nodded and took a few steps back. "It always is a bit stuffy in the greenhouse, which is one of the reasons I don't like workin' here."

"What would you rather be doin'?"

"Fishin'. . .bird-watchin'. . .almost anything outdoors," she answered, giving him another one of her dimpled smiles.

Silas swallowed hard. If he was ever going to ask her, he'd better do it quick, because right now he felt like racing for the door and heading straight home.

"The reason I stopped by was to see if ya might wanna go to Paradise Lake with me tomorrow. Your brother Joseph and me were talkin' the other day, and he mentioned that ya like to fish. So, I thought maybe we could do a bit of fishin', and if we're lucky, get in some bird-watchin', too." There, it was out. Now all he had to do was wait for her answer.

Rachel stood there, staring at him like she was in some kind of a daze. For a minute he wondered if he would need to repeat himself.

"Since tomorrow is an off Sunday and there won't be no preachin' service, I guess it'd be as good a time as any for some outdoor fun," she said in a quavery voice.

He jumped up. "You mean you'll go?"

She nodded. "I'd be happy to. How 'bout I fix us a picnic lunch to take along? Fishin' always makes me real hungry, and later tonight I was plannin' to bake some more of those chocolate chip cookies you like so well."

Silas licked his lips in anticipation of what was to come. He was mighty glad he'd finally gotten up the nerve to ask Rachel to go fishing. "Let's meet at the lake around nine o'clock. How's that sound?"

"Sounds *gut* to me," she said, walking him to the door.

❧

Rachel stood at the window, watching Silas's buggy disappear down the lane. When it was well out of sight, she hugged herself real tight and started whirling around the room. "I can't believe it! Silas Swartley and I are goin' fishin'!"

She couldn't help but wonder, and yes, even hope that this sudden invitation was a sign that Silas was beginning to care for her. *Guess maybe he's not interested in Pauline after all.* She laughed out loud. "Maybe I'd better start fillin' my hope chest with a few more things. If Silas enjoys my company tomorrow, he might even offer to take me home from the next singin'. Now that would mean we were courtin'!" She would have to remember to thank Joseph for letting Silas know how much she liked to fish.

                                    ða

As soon as Silas returned home, he went straight to the barn to get out his fishing gear. Tomorrow he would be meeting Rachel at Paradise Lake. Besides the fishing pole, several fat worms, extra tackle, and line, he'd decided to take along his binoculars and the new book he'd recently bought on bird-watching.

He grinned as he grabbed his pole off the wall. It amazed him that any woman would actually like to fish and study birds, but he was glad he and Rachel had that in common. None of his brothers showed the least bit of interest in either birds or fishing with him, and now that Reuben was gone, he had been forced to fish alone.

Silas frowned deeply. He hadn't thought about Reuben for several weeks, and he wished he wasn't thinking of him right now. Reminders of Reuben always made him think about Anna, and he wasn't sure he was completely over her yet. He had loved her a lot, and she'd hurt him real bad, running off with his best friend and all. A fellow didn't get over being kicked in the gut like that overnight. Matters of the heart took time to heal, and until a moment ago, he thought his heart was on the way to mending.

"I'll feel better once I'm seated on the dock at Paradise Lake with my fishin' pole in the water and the warm sun against my back," he muttered.

"Who ya talkin' to, Silas?"

Silas whirled around. There stood his youngest brother, Sam, looking up at him like he was a fly on the wall. "I ain't talkin' to no one but myself, and you shouldn't go around sneakin' up on others," he scolded.

Sam scrunched up his freckled nose. "I weren't sneakin'.

Just came out to the barn to feed the cats, and I heard you talkin' about goin' fishin'."

Silas nodded. "That's right. I'll be headed to Paradise Lake in the morning."

"Can I go along?" Sam asked eagerly.

Silas gave his brother a little pat on the arm. "Naw, I'd rather go alone. Besides, you don't even like to fish."

"I know, but it might be better than hangin' around here all day. Ever since Mom got that cast on her arm, she's been askin' me to do more chores."

"Ball wollt's besser geh—soon it will go better," Silas said with a grin. "Mom won't always be wearin' her arm in a sling."

Sam shrugged. "I guess you're right." He turned to go, calling over his shoulder, "If it's a girl you're meetin' tomorrow, could ya save me a piece of cake from the picnic?"

Silas ran his fingers through the back of his hair. That little brother of his was sure no dumb bunny. Only thing was, it wouldn't be cake he'd be bringing home tomorrow, because Rachel had said she was going to bake his favorite kind of cookie.

eleven

Rachel had a hard time getting away Sunday morning without telling her family she was meeting Silas at the lake. She tried to be discreet when she packed the picnic lunch, hoping no one would notice how much she had stashed inside the wicker basket. Both Elizabeth and Perry asked if they could go along, and she almost felt guilty telling them no. If she and Silas were going to get better acquainted, the last thing she needed was her rowdy brother and nosy sister tagging along.

The morning sun slid from behind a cloud as Rachel hitched the horse to the buggy. It was a bit chilly out, but the day held a promise of sunshine. She was about to climb into the driver's seat when Dad called out to her. "I'm not so sure I like the idea of you goin' to the lake by yourself."

"I've been fishin' there since I was a *kinder,* and I've never had a problem," she replied. "Besides, there's usually plenty of people around, so I probably won't be alone."

Dad shook his head. "That may be, but it ain't *gut* for a young woman to be runnin' around by herself. I really think you should take your sister or one of your brothers along."

Rachel placed the picnic basket under the front seat and turned to face her father. "I'm meetin' someone."

He gave his beard a few good yanks. "Ah, so my daughter has a beau now, does she?"

Rachel felt the heat of a blush stain her cheeks. "He's not a beau, just a friend."

Dad chuckled. "So it is a fellow you're meetin' then?"

She nodded. *"Jah."*

"Mind if I ask who?"

"It's Silas Swartley."

Dad's smile widened. "A fine young man, Silas is." He winked at Rachel. "Should I be askin' your *mamm* to start makin' a weddin' quilt?"

"Himmel!" Rachel exclaimed. "I knew I shouldn't have said anything. Like I stated before, Silas and I are just friends."

"Then why the big secret 'bout meetin' him?"

Rachel hung her head. "I–I—just didn't want anyone jumpin' to conclusions."

Dad gave her arm a gentle pat. "Your secret's safe with me, Daughter. Now run along and catch plenty of fish, will ya? Some nice, tasty trout would look mighty *gut* on the supper table!"

Rachel smiled and climbed into the buggy. She was ever so glad her *daed* was such a thoughtful man.

&

Silas was sitting on the dock with his fishing line dangling in the water. There were several small boats on the lake, but no one else was on the dock or shoreline. Maybe he and Rachel would be alone all day. Did he really want to be alone with her? He'd thought he did yesterday when he asked her to meet him here. Now that he'd had ample time to think about it, he worried that he might have been a bit hasty making the invitation. What if Rachel thought he was interested in her as more than a friend? What if she thought this was a real date?

Silas stared out across the lake, his gaze settling on a crop of trees where several crows sat, making their distinctive call of *caw, caw, caw!* Truth be told, he really did enjoy Rachel's company. The fact that she liked birds and fishing was a benefit, but it was her sweet spirit and appreciation for the simple things in life that really captured his attention.

"She ain't too bad lookin', either," Silas said aloud. He closed his eyes, and Rachel's pleasant face flashed into his mind. Her pale blue eyes and soft, straw-colored hair made her appear almost angelic. And whenever she smiled, those cute little dimples made him want to reach right out and touch her cheeks.

Silas shook his head. *What am I thinkin'? Rachel is Anna's little sister. She's five years younger than me and ain't much more'n a* kinder. *Of course, I do know of some married couples where one is older than the other.* He sighed deeply. *Guess five years ain't really all that much.*

Silas was driven from his inner conflict when he heard a horse and buggy come plodding up the road. He turned and waved as Rachel's buggy pulled into the grassy spot near the dock.

❧

Rachel smiled and waved at Silas, who was sitting on the edge of the dock holding a fishing pole. He looked so eager. Was it possible that he was as happy to see her as she was to see him? She prayed it was so.

"Catch anything yet?" she asked as she stepped down from the buggy.

Silas shook his head. "Not yet, but then I haven't been here very long."

Rachel grabbed her fishing pole from the back of the buggy, along with the can of night crawlers she'd caught last night. When she walked onto the dock, Silas slid over, making room for her to sit beside him. "Sure is a nice day," he remarked. "Should have our share of trout in no time." He winked at Rachel and her heart skipped a beat.

Does he have some feelings for me? she asked herself. It was a glimmer of hope she would cling to.

The sun was shining brightly, the sky was a clear aquamarine, and the lake was smooth as glass. Rachel felt a sense of peace settle over her as she cast out her line. It felt so right being here with Silas. If only. . . *No, I mustn't allow myself to start daydreamin'. Today, I'm just gonna relax and enjoy the company of the man I could surely spend the rest of my life with.*

By noon, Silas had caught six trout and four bass, and Rachel had five of each. They both cleaned their own catch, then put the fish inside the small coolers they'd brought along.

"I don't know about you, but I'm starvin'," Silas said, eyeing the picnic basket Rachel had taken from the buggy and placed upon the quilt she'd spread on the ground.

"I made plenty, so I'm glad you're hungry," she said with a smile.

Silas dropped to the quilt. "What'd ya bring?"

Rachel knelt next to the picnic basket and opened the lid. "Let's see now. . .ham and cheese sandwiches, dill pickle slices, macaroni salad, cheese curds, pickled beet eggs, iced tea to drink, and for dessert. . .chocolate chip cookies."

Silas licked his lips. "Yum. Let's pray, then we'll eat ourselves full!"

Rachel and Silas shared stories, told jokes, and got to know each other better. By the time they finished eating the last of the cookies, Rachel felt as though she'd known Silas all her life. Actually, she had, but not on such a personal level. Silas, being five years her senior, had always hung around her older sister, so she'd never had the chance to learn what many of his likes and dislikes were. Today he'd shared his aversion to liver and onions, a dish his *mamm* seemed intent on fixing at least once a month. He also revealed his objection to so many Amish parents who chose to look the other way when their rebellious teenagers sowed their wild oats. Silas talked about his relationship to God and how he'd been praying for the Lord to have His will in his life.

"Yep, I believe strongly in prayer," Silas said with obvious conviction. "It's the key to each new day and the lock for every night."

Rachel smiled. "You're right about that." Even as she said

the words, Rachel wondered if she was being sincere. Oh, she believed in prayer, all right. The problem was, she didn't pray as often as she should anymore. Since she'd been busy helping Silas's mother, Rachel had let her personal devotions and prayer time slip. It was something she needed to work on, and right then she promised herself and God that she would.

Silas chewed on a blade of grass as he began telling Rachel what he thought about so many *younga* who, because they were allowed to taste some worldly things, had gone English.

"I think it's a sin and a shame," he said with feeling. "If I ever have any *kinder,* I'm gonna hold a tight rein on 'em so's they don't ever leave the faith."

Rachel leaned back on her elbows and let his words digest fully before she answered. "You might be right, but then again, holdin' a tight rein could turn someone's head in the opposite direction." She sat up and pivoted to face him. "Take a baby robin, for example. If its *mamm* never taught it to fly and always kept it protected inside the nest, do you think that *buppli* would ever learn to soar in the air?"

Silas scratched the back of his head and squinted his dark eyes. "I guess you've got a point. You're pretty bright for someone so young."

Rachel felt as though Silas had slapped her on the face with a wet rag. *Why'd he have to go and bring up my age? And just when we were beginnin' to have such a good time.* "I'll have you know, Silas Swartley," she asserted, "I'll be nineteen next Saturday. My *mamm* was married by the time she was my age, and—"

Silas held up one hand. "Whoa, now! Don't get your feathers all ruffled. I sure didn't mean to offend ya."

Rachel grabbed their empty paper plates and the plastic containers the food had been in and began slinging them into the picnic basket. Her face felt hot, her hands were shaking, and tears were stinging the backs of her eyes. She had so wanted this day to be perfect. Maybe she was too sensitive. Might could be that Silas hadn't meant to upset her at all. She stood and proceeded to move toward her buggy. "Guess I should be gettin' back home."

Silas jumped up and ran after her. "You can't go now, Rachel. We haven't spent any time lookin' at birds."

She shrugged. "Maybe some other time. I'm not much in the mood anymore."

Silas placed a restraining hand on Rachel's arm. "Please, don't go. I'm awful sorry for makin' ya mad."

She swallowed hard, struggling to keep her tears at bay. Silas was looking at her with those big brown eyes, and he really did look sorry. "I'm not exactly mad," she admitted. "I just get tired of everyone thinkin' I'm still a *kinder.*" Her arms made a wide arc as she motioned toward the lake. "Could a child catch as many fish as I did today?" Before Silas had a chance to answer, she rushed on. "Could a little girl have fixed such a tasty picnic lunch or baked a batch of cookies you couldn't eat enough of?"

Silas studied her a few seconds, then in an unexpected gesture, he pulled her to his chest. "No, Rachel, only a feisty young woman coulda done all those things."

Rachel held her breath as he moved his fingers in gentle, soothing circles across her back. Was Silas about to kiss her? She wrapped her arms around his neck and nestled her head against his shoulder.

Then, as quickly as he'd embraced her, Silas pulled away. "Now that we've got that cleared up, how's about I get my binoculars and bird identification book, and the two of us can spend the next hour or so lookin' for some unusual feathered creatures?"

Rachel nodded as a sense of embarrassment rattled through her. Silas's sudden shift in mood hit her like a blow to the stomach and she cringed, wondering what he must have thought about her brazen actions. Even though it was Silas who initiated the hug, she had taken it one step further. Truth be told, Silas had never led her to believe he had any romantic feelings for her. The embrace was probably just a friendly, brotherly gesture.

"You get your gear, and I'll put away the picnic stuff," she said, scooting quickly away, before he could see how red her face must be.

A short time later, Silas and Rachel were seated on the grass, taking turns looking through his binoculars, as though their physical encounter had never even taken place. In no time at all they'd spotted several gray catbirds, a brown thrasher, a few mourning doves, and several species of ducks on the lake. Silas looked each one up in his bird identification book, and they discussed the various traits and habitats of those they'd seen.

"Do you have a bird book or binoculars of your own?" Silas asked.

Rachel shook her head. "Whenever I save up enough money, some other need always seems to come along, so I just jot notes on a paper about all the interestin' birds I see." She was tempted to tell him that here lately, she'd spent most of her money buying more things for her hope chest, but she thought better of bringing that subject up. Silas might think she was hinting at marriage, and she wasn't about to say or do anything that would spoil the rest of the day. Except for that one misunderstanding, their time together had been almost perfect. Even if she never got to be alone with Silas again, she would always cherish the memory of this day.

Closing her eyes, Rachel uttered a brief, silent prayer. *It's been a* wunderbaar *day, Lord. Danki.*

twelve

After their enjoyable day at the lake, Rachel expected Silas to be friendlier the following week. He wasn't. In fact, she saw very little of him, and when he did come to the house for meals, he seemed aloof and kind of cranky whenever someone spoke to him. Something wasn't right. She felt it in every fiber of her being. She wanted to ask him what was wrong, but there never seemed to be a good time, what with his family always around.

By Saturday, Rachel was fit to be tied. She'd been forced to stay home from the Swartleys' again because Mom and Dad went to town for more supplies. That meant she was needed at the greenhouse, and even worse, it appeared as though her family had forgotten all about her birthday. Not one person said "happy birthday" during breakfast, and there was no sign of any gifts, either. It was such a disappointment not to be remembered on her special day.

Elizabeth and Perry had been left home this time, and they were still up at the house when Rachel walked out to the greenhouse. She put the OPEN sign in the window, lit all the kerosene lanterns, and made a small fire in the wood-burning stove to take the autumn chill out of the room.

Rachel studied her surroundings, letting her gaze travel from the plants hanging by the rafters on long chains to the small wooden pots and lawn figurines sitting on shelves. Dad had made most of those things, and his expertise with wood was quite evident. Rachel knew her folks loved this greenhouse, and she was also aware that it had been one of the things that brought them together. Even so, she had no desire to spend so much time helping out here. Today, of all days, she would much rather be outside.

"It's my birthday," she fumed. "I should at least be allowed the pleasure of a walk to the river." She plunked down on the stool behind the counter, placed her elbows on the hard wood, and rested her chin in the palms of her hands.

Pauline showed up a few minutes later, and Joseph was with her.

"I thought you were out in the barn," Rachel said, giving her brother a knowing look.

He shrugged, and his face turned kind of pink. "I was, 'til I saw Pauline's buggy come down the lane."

"Are ya plannin' to help out here today?" Rachel asked hopefully. "If so, maybe I won't be needed."

"I wish I could, but it's not possible today." Joseph cast a quick glance in Pauline's direction, then looked back at Rachel with a silly grin on his face.

"What are ya doin' here, if it's not to work?" Rachel asked impatiently.

"I came to see Pauline. That is, if you have no objections."

Pauline chuckled and elbowed Joseph in the ribs. He laughed and jabbed her right back.

At least somebody's happy today, Rachel thought ruefully. "I think I'll go in the back room and see if any of the plants need waterin'," she announced.

"Okay, sure," Joseph said, never taking his eyes off Pauline.

"Sickenin'. Downright sickenin'," Rachel muttered under her breath as she headed for the middle section of the greenhouse. *This day can't be over soon enough to suit me!*

❧

Silas paced back and forth in front of his open courting buggy. Should he or shouldn't he make this trip? Would his intentions be misrepresented? What exactly were his intentions, anyway? He'd spent the last week trying to sort out his feelings, and yet he felt more confused now than ever.

Pushing his troubled thoughts aside, he tried to pray. God seemed so far away today, but he knew it was his own fault. He'd been negligent in reading the Bible this morning, and his only prayer had been the silent one before breakfast.

I won't allow myself to move away from You, Lord, Silas prayed. *I'd never want to end up like Reuben and Anna, who obviously fell away.* Silas was reminded that up until six months ago, he and Reuben had been close. It was as much a surprise to Silas as it had been to Reuben's folks when they discovered Reuben had gone "fancy."

Then there was Anna. Beautiful, spirited, stubborn Anna. Silas had been in love with her since the first grade, when they'd started attending school in the Amish one-room schoolhouse. In his mind's eye, he could still see the back of her cute little head. He'd sat in the desk behind her for all of the eight years they'd gone to school. Anna, with her dazzling green eyes and hair the color of ripe peaches. She'd stolen his heart when he was six years old, and she'd broken it in two when he was twenty-three. Would he ever be free of the pain? Would the image of her lovely face be forever etched in his mind? Could he learn to trust another woman?

It does no good to pine for what you can't have, a little voice reminded. *Get on with your life and follow Me.*

Silas moved to the front of the buggy, where his faithful horse waited patiently. He leaned against the gelding's side and stroked his silky ears. "What do ya say, old boy? Do we take a little ride, or do we stay home?"

The horse whinnied as if in response, and Silas smiled. "All right then, let's be on our way."

❧

Rachel had just put the CLOSED sign in the window and was about to turn down the lights when she heard a horse and buggy pull up in front of the greenhouse. Pauline had gone home fifteen minutes ago, and Rachel was anxious to head home herself. She sighed deeply. "Guess I can handle one more customer."

Rachel opened the front door, and her mouth dropped open when she saw Silas standing there holding a paper bag in one hand and a bouquet of orange and yellow chrysanthemums in the other.

"Well, well," she said with a giggle, "it isn't every day someone shows up at the greenhouse carryin' a bunch of flowers."

Silas chuckled. "Guess that's true enough. Most folks leave here with flowers, but it ain't likely they'd be bringing 'em in."

Rachel stepped aside to allow Silas entrance. "So what brings you here at closin' time, Silas Swartley?"

He cleared his throat real loud, then handed her the flowers and paper sack. "Just wanted to give you these. Happy birthday, Rachel."

Rachel felt as though all the breath had been squeezed clean out of her lungs. This was such a surprise. Never in a million years had she expected a gift from Silas, especially since he'd been so distant all week. *"Danki,"* she murmured. "How'd ya know today was my birthday?"

"You said somethin' about it when we went fishin' last Sunday," he replied.

Rachel placed the flowers on the counter and opened the paper sack. She let out a little squeal when she looked inside. "Binoculars and a bird watchin' book? Oh, Silas, this is my best present!" The truth was, it was her only birthday present, but she wasn't about to tell him that. It was bad enough her whole family had forgotten her special day; she sure didn't want to talk about it.

"I was hopin' ya might like it," Silas said, taking a few steps closer to Rachel. "Now, whenever you see some unusual bird, you can look it up in the book and find out all about its habits and whatnot."

Rachel withdrew the binoculars. "These will sure come in handy, too."

Silas nodded. *"Jah,* I often put my own binoculars to *gut* use."

Rachel swallowed hard. Why was Silas looking at her so funny? Did that gentle expression in his dark eyes and the agreeable smile on his clean-shaven face mean anything more than just friendship? She sure couldn't come right out and ask, but she needed to know if she dared to hope.

As if he sensed her dilemma, Silas reached out and took Rachel's hand. "I really enjoyed our time of fishin' and lookin' at birds the other day. If the weather holds out, maybe we can find time to do it again."

Rachel flicked her tongue back and forth across her lower lip. The sensation of Silas's touch did funny things to her insides. "I'd surely like that," she murmured. "I had a *gut* time last week, too."

Silas let go of her hand, then turned and moved slowly toward the door. "Well, guess I should be gettin' on home. Mom's probably got supper ready."

Rachel nodded. "I need to go up to the house and see about fixin' our supper as well. My folks went to town this mornin', and they still aren't back yet, so I'd better be sure there's somethin' ready to eat when they do get home."

When Silas got to the door, he turned and said, "I hear tell there's gonna be a singin' over at Abner Lapp's place two weeks from tomorrow. Do ya think ya might go?"

"Maybe." Rachel shrugged. "If I can get Joseph to take me."

Silas grinned. "From what I hear, your brother's got a pretty *gut* reason to bring his courtin' buggy to a singin'. My guess is, he'll be there."

Rachel nodded. "You're probably right."

Silas opened the door. "Well, see ya at preachin' tomorrow, Rachel." He bounded off the porch and climbed into his buggy before Rachel could say anything more.

She smiled to herself. "Guess this wasn't such a bad birthday after all."

❧

Holding her bouquet of flowers and the paper sack Silas had given her, Rachel stepped into the darkened kitchen. She had barely closed the door when a kerosene light flickered on and a chorus of voices yelled, "Happy birthday!"

"What in the world?" Rachel's mouth fell open as she studied her surroundings. Mom, Dad, Joseph, Perry, and Elizabeth all sat at the table, which was fully set for supper. On one end of the cupboard was a chocolate cake, and beside it were several gifts wrapped in plain, brown paper.

"Elizabeth, did you do all this?" Rachel asked her sister.

Elizabeth smiled. "I helped, but Mama did most of it."

Rachel's eyebrows drew together. "How could that be? Mom and Dad have been gone all day."

Mom grinned like a cat that had just chased down a fat little mouse. "Came back early. Just so we could surprise ya."

"But I never heard your buggy come down the lane," Rachel argued. "I don't see how—"

Dad chuckled. "We used the old road comin' into the back of our property."

Tears stung the back of Rachel's eyes and she blinked to keep them from spilling over. Her folks really did care. They hadn't forgotten it was her birthday after all.

"What's that you've got in your hands?" The question came from Perry, and Rachel felt her face heat with embarrassment.

"It's—uh—a birthday present."

"From who?" Joseph asked, giving her a discerning look.

"Silas Swartley," she said, trying to keep her voice from quivering.

"Rachel's got a boyfriend! Rachel's got a boyfriend!" Elizabeth taunted.

"I do not!"

"Do so!"

"Silas is just a *gut* friend," Rachel argued. "That oughtta be clear as anythin'."

Joseph raised his eyebrows. "Oh sure—about as clear as mud. He's a *gut* friend all right. One who gives you a birthday present and takes you fishin'."

Rachel turned to face her father, giving him an accusing look. He shook his head. "He didn't hear it from me."

Mom shook her finger at Dad. "You knew our daughter had gone fishin' with Silas Swartley and you never said a word?"

"Rachel asked me not to say anything."

"If Dad didn't mention it, then how'd you know?" Rachel asked, looking back at Joseph.

He shrugged. "There were some other folks out at Paradise Lake, ya know."

"We never talked to anyone else," Rachel said quickly. "In fact, we were the only ones on the dock."

"That may be true, but there were some boats out on the water," Joseph reminded.

"Spies, don'tcha mean?" Rachel declared. "Humph! Some folks need to keep their big mouths shut where others are concerned."

"Now, don't go gettin' yourself into a snit," Mom said soothingly. "There was no harm done, so come sit yourself down and eat your favorite supper."

Rachel had to admit, the fried chicken and mashed potatoes did look mighty good. She was real hungry, too. She may as well eat this special supper Mom and Elizabeth had worked so hard to prepare. She would have a serious talk with Joseph later on. Then she'd find out who the informer had been.

thirteen

Rachel sat on the edge of her bed, looking over the presents she'd received earlier that day. It had been a *gut* birthday, even if Joseph had let the cat out of the bag about her and Silas going fishing together. Joseph told her later that it was Amon Zook who'd spilled the beans. He'd been fishing on the lake with his son, Ben.

She chuckled softly. "Guess ya can't keep anything secret these days."

Focusing on her gifts again, Rachel studied the set of hand-made pillowcases Mom had given her and insisted must go straight into Rachel's hope chest. Dad's gift was a new oil lamp—also a hope chest item, since she already had two perfectly good lamps in her bedroom. Joseph and Perry had gone together on a box of cream-filled chocolates, which Rachel had generously shared with the family. Elizabeth had made several handkerchiefs. Then there was her favorite gift of all— the binoculars and bird identification book Silas had given her. The candy was almost gone. The handkerchiefs would be useful in the days to come. The oil lamp and pillowcases might never be used if Rachel didn't get married. Silas's gift, on the other hand, was something she would use whenever she studied birds in their yard and the surrounding area.

Rachel scooted off the bed and stepped around the cedar chest at the end of her bed, opened the lid, and slipped the pillowcases and lamp inside. She hadn't given her hope chest much thought until recently. Now that Silas was being so friendly, there might be a ray of hope for her future. " 'But I will hope continually, and will yet praise thee more and more,' " she murmured. "Thank You, Lord, for such a *gut* day."

As Rachel closed the lid of the chest, she caught sight of Anna's hope chest in the corner of her room. She was tempted to open it and look through its contents, but she thought better of it. It belonged to her sister, and she still didn't feel right about snooping through Anna's personal things.

She did give the hope chest to you, her inner voice reminded. Rachel was about to go over and open it up, but she changed her mind. What if Anna should ever return to the Amish faith? Wouldn't she want her hope chest back?

Someday, if Rachel should ever become *published,* then there would be a use for the things in both hers and Anna's hope chests. She would wait awhile to see what was inside. In the meantime, she planned to start adding even more things to her own hope chest.

ॐ

Silas felt a sense of excitement as he prepared to go to the singing that was to be held in Abner Lapp's barn. There would be a big bonfire and enough eats to fill even the hungriest man's stomach. Neither the singing, bonfire, nor even all the food was the reason he was looking forward to going. Simply put, Silas wanted to see Rachel again.

Silas climbed into his freshly cleaned courting buggy. His heartbeat quickened as he picked up the reins. The more time he spent with Rachel, the more he was drawn to her. Was it merely because they had so much in common, or was there something more going on? Could he possibly being falling for little Rachel Beachy, in spite of their age difference or the fact that she was the sister of his first love?

He shook his head and moved the horse forward. "I'd better take my time with Rachel, hadn't I, old boy? Elsewise, there might be *Kein Ausgang*—no exit for either one of us."

ॐ

Fifty young people milled about the Lapps' barn, eating,

playing games, and visiting. The singing had already taken place, so the rest of the evening would be spent in pleasant camaraderie.

Rachel and Joseph had gone their separate ways as soon as they arrived, she with some other woman her age, and Joseph with Pauline Hostetler. That really wasn't such a big surprise, since he'd been hanging around her so much lately.

Rachel had just finished eating a sandwich and had taken a seat on a bale of straw, planning to relax and watch the couples around her. She was pretty sure her brother would be asking to take Pauline home tonight, and it had her kind of worried. What if he wanted to be alone with his date? What if he expected Rachel to find another way home? It would be rather embarrassing if she had to go begging for a ride.

She scanned the many faces inside the barn, trying to decide who might be the best choice to ask, should it become necessary. Her gaze fell on Silas Swartley, talking with a group of young men near the food table. It would be bold to ask him for a ride, even if they had become friends over the past few months. It was a fellow's place to invite a girl to ride in his courting buggy, not the other way around. Besides, she hadn't seen much of Silas lately. Every day last week, when she'd been at his place helping out, Silas had been busy with the fall harvest. They hadn't had a real conversation since a week ago Saturday, when Silas dropped by the greenhouse to give her a birthday present.

Rachel noticed Abe Lapp sitting by himself, eating a huge piece of chocolate cake. Abe was the same age as Rachel, and they'd known each other a long time. She could ask him for a lift home, but there was just one problem. . .Abe lived right here. He wouldn't be driving his horse and buggy anywhere tonight.

"Seen any interestin' birds lately?"

The question took Rachel by surprise. She'd been in such a

dilemma over who to ask for a ride, she hadn't even noticed that Silas Swartley was standing right beside her. She glanced up and smiled. *"Jah."*

Silas pulled up another bale of straw and sat down. "You like my birthday present?"

She nodded. "A whole lot."

"Mom's gettin' her cast off soon. Guess ya won't be comin' around so much anymore," he said, looking down at his hands, clasped together in his lap.

Rachel studied him a moment before she answered. Did she detect a note of sadness in his voice when he mentioned her not coming over anymore, or was it just wishful thinking? If Silas knew how much she loved him yet didn't have feelings for her, the humiliation would be too great to bear. "I–I'm glad I could help out, but things will soon be back to normal at your house, so—"

"Rachel, would ya like some hot chocolate and then go sit with me out by the bonfire?" Abe Lapp interrupted as he plunked down on the same bale of straw Rachel was sitting on.

Silas's jaw clenched, and he shot Abe a look that could only be interpreted as one of irritation. "Rachel and I were havin' a little talk, Abe. If she wants anything, I'll be happy to fetch it for her."

Rachel stirred uneasily. What was going on here? If she hadn't known better, she'd have believed Silas was jealous of Abe Lapp. But that was ridiculous. Abe and Rachel were just friends, the same as she and Silas. Abe was only being nice by asking if she wanted some hot chocolate. Surely he wasn't interested in her in a romantic kind of way.

Abe poked Rachel on the shoulder. "What do you say? Would ya like me to get ya somethin' to drink?"

Silas jumped up quickly, nearly tripping over his bale of straw. "Didn't ya hear what I said? If Rachel wants anything, I'll get it for her!"

Rachel's heart was thumping so hard she feared it might burst wide open. Why was Silas acting so upset? It made no sense at all.

Abe stood up, too. "Don'tcha think that's Rachel's decision?"

Silas pivoted toward Rachel. "Well? Who's gonna get the hot chocolate?"

Rachel gulped. Were they really going to force her to choose? She cleared her throat, then offered them both a brief smile. "Me. I'll get my own drink, thank you very much." With that said, she hopped up and sprinted off toward the refreshment table.

❧

Silas looked at Abe and chuckled. "Guess we've been outsmarted."

Abe shrugged and reached up to rub the back of his neck. "I think so." He started to move away but stopped after he'd taken a few steps. "Look, Silas, if Rachel and you are courtin', I'll back off. If not, then she's fair game, and I plan on makin' my move."

Silas's eyes widened. "Your move?" Heat boiled up his spine as jealousy seared through him like hot coals on the fire.

Abe nodded. "I thought I might ask her to go fishin' with me sometime."

"Fishin'?"

"Yeah. I hear tell Rachel likes to fish."

"Where'd ya hear that?"

"Someone saw her at Paradise Lake a few weeks ago. She was sittin' on the dock with her fishin' pole."

Silas leveled Abe with a look he hoped would end this conversation. "That was me she was fishin' with."

"So, you two *are* courtin'."

Silas clenched his fists. It wasn't in his nature to want to hit someone, and everything about fighting went against the Amish way, but right now he was struggling with the impulse to punch Abe Lapp right in the nose. What was the fellow trying to do—goad him into an argument or a fistfight? He'd always considered Abe to be nice enough, but up until a few moments ago he hadn't realized Abe was interested in Rachel.

Silas was still trying to decide how to deal with Abe Lapp when Rachel returned, carrying a mug of steaming hot chocolate and a piece of shoofly pie. She smiled sweetly at both of them, then seated herself on the bale of straw.

Silas leaned over so his face was mere inches from Rachel's. Her pale blue eyes seemed to probe his innermost being, and Silas felt his heart begin to hammer. With no further thought, he blurted out, "I'd like to take ya home in my courtin' buggy tonight, Rachel. Would ya be willin' to go?"

She took a little sip of her drink, glanced up at Abe, then back over at Silas and replied, *"Jah,* I will."

Now that Rachel had accepted his invitation, Silas wasn't sure how he felt. Had he asked merely to get under Abe's skin? He looked down at Rachel, sitting there so sweet and innocent, and he knew the answer to his troubling question. He really did want to take her home. He enjoyed her company, maybe a bit more than he cared to admit. The truth was, Anna had hurt him real bad, and there was still a part of him that was afraid Rachel might do the same thing.

Silas's disconcerting thoughts were jolted away when Abe slapped him on the back. *"Jah, well, Ich bins Zufreide*—all right, I am satisfied." With that, Abe walked away, leaving Silas and Rachel alone.

"What time were you plannin' to head for home?" Rachel asked as Silas took a seat on the other bale of straw.

He shrugged. "Whenever you're done eatin' your pie and hot chocolate, I suppose."

"Aren't ya gonna have some?"

He chuckled. "I already had enough food for three fellows my size."

Rachel finished the rest of her dessert and stood up. "Guess I'd better find Joseph and tell him I won't be riding home in his buggy tonight."

Silas reached for her empty plate and mug. "I'll put this away for you while you go lookin' for him."

"Danki," she said, offering him a heart-melting smile. He sure hoped he hadn't made a big mistake asking to take her home. What if she jumped to the wrong conclusions? What if she thought that one buggy ride meant they were officially courting?

You didn't have to ask her, a voice in him reminded. *You could have conceded to Abe Lapp.* Silas gritted his teeth. *Never!*

❧

Rachel found her brother outside by the bonfire, talking with Pauline Hostetler. She quickly explained that she'd be riding home with Silas, and Joseph seemed almost relieved.

"No problem. No problem, a'tall," he said, looking down at his boots.

Rachel bit back a smile. She knew it would probably rile Joseph if she questioned him about whether he planned to escort anyone home, but she had to ask.

"You takin' anyone special home tonight?" she whispered in his ear.

In the light of the fire, she saw his face flame as he nodded. *"Jah,* Pauline."

"That's *gut.* I'm glad to hear it." She turned and waved. "See you at home."

Joseph waved back. "Yeah, later."

Rachel practically skipped back to the barn. Joseph had a girlfriend, and she was going home in Silas's courting buggy. Life was *wunderbaar,* and she felt deliriously happy!

fourteen

A sense of exhilaration shot through Rachel as she sat in Silas's open buggy with the crisp wind whipping against her face. She chanced a peek at her escort, hoping he, too, was enjoying the ride.

Silas grinned back at her. "I think I smell winter in the air. Won't be too awfully long and we can take out the sleigh."

We? Does he mean me and him goin' for a sleigh ride? Rachel closed her eyes and tried to picture herself snuggled beneath a warm quilt, snow falling in huge, white flakes, and the sound of sleigh bells jingling in the chilly air.

"What are you thinkin' about?" Silas asked, breaking into her musings.

Rachel's eyes snapped open. "Oh, winter. . .sleigh bells. . . snow."

Silas chuckled. "Don't forget hot apple cider and pumpkin bread. Nothin' tastes better after a sleigh ride than a big mug of cider and several thick hunks of Mom's spicy pumpkin bread."

"My favorite winter snack is popcorn, apple slices, and hot chocolate with plenty of marshmallows," Rachel interjected.

"I like those things, too." Silas snickered. "Guess there ain't much in the way of food I don't like." Reaching into his jacket pocket, he withdrew a chunk of black licorice. "Want some?"

Rachel shook her head. "No thanks." She studied him as he began chewing the candy. In spite of his hearty appetite, there wasn't an ounce of fat on Silas. He was all muscle—no doubt from doing so many farm chores. *I'd love him no matter how he looked,* Rachel mused. It wasn't hard to picture herself and Silas sitting on the front porch of their own home, looking through binoculars and talking about all the birds nesting in their backyard.

She shook her head, as though to bring some sense of reason into her thinking. Silas was a friend, and he'd offered her a ride home from the singing. That sure didn't mean he had thoughts of romance or marriage on his mind. She couldn't allow herself to fantasize about it, even if she did want more than friendship. She loved Silas so much, and each moment they spent together only made her more sure of it. She didn't want to feel this way; it wasn't safe for her heart. But no matter how hard she tried, Rachel couldn't seem to keep from hoping that Silas would someday declare his love for her.

As they pulled into Rachel's farmyard, she released a deep sigh, wishing the ride didn't have to end so soon. If only they could keep on going. If only. . .

Silas halted the horse near the barn and turned in his seat to face Rachel. "Thanks for lettin' me bring ya home tonight. I enjoyed the ride a whole lot more than if I'd been alone."

"Me, too," she freely admitted.

"You're a special girl, Rachel. I can see why Abe Lapp would be interested in you."

Rachel's breath caught in her throat, and her cheeks burned with embarrassment. The admiration in Silas's voice sounded so genuine. His gaze dropped to her lips. For one heart-stopping moment, Rachel had the crazy idea of throwing herself into his arms and begging him to love her. She knew better than to let her emotions run wild. She had too much pride to throw herself at him.

"Sure you don't want some licorice?" Silas asked, giving her a crooked grin.

All she could do was shake her head, her thoughts so lost in the darkness of his ebony eyes, where the moonlight reflected like a pool of clear water.

Rachel's heart pulsated as Silas slipped his arms around

her waist and pulled her closer. She tipped her head back and savored the sweet smell of licorice as his lips met hers in a kiss so pleasing it almost lifted her right off the buggy seat. This was her first real kiss, and she could only hope her inexperience wasn't evident as she kissed him back with all the emotion welling up within her soul.

Silas pulled away suddenly, looking shaken and confused. "Rachel, I'm so sorry, I—"

Rachel held up her hand, feeling as though a glass of cold water had been dashed in her face. "Please, don't say anything more." She hopped down from the buggy and sprinted toward the house, as the ache of humiliation bore down on her like a heavy blanket of snow. She wasn't sure why Silas had kissed her, but one thing was certain—he was sorry he had.

≈

All the way home Silas kept berating himself. *Why did I kiss Rachel like that? She must think I'm off in the head to be doin' something so brazen on our first buggy ride.*

As Silas thought more on it, he realized as much as he'd enjoyed the kiss, it hadn't been fair to lead Rachel on. She might think because he took her home, then went so far as to kiss her, it meant they were a couple and would be courting from now on.

"Is that what it means?" he said aloud. Did he want to court Rachel Beachy? Was he feeling more than friendship for her, or did he only want to be with her because she reminded him of Anna?

Silas slapped the side of his head. "What am I sayin'? Rachel's nothin' like her older sister. Nothin' a'tall. Guess I'd better commit the whole thing to prayer. I sure enough wasn't expecting this to happen tonight, and I definitely don't have any answers."

≈

For the next two weeks, Rachel helped out at the Swartleys', and for the next two weeks, she did everything she could to avoid Silas. It made her sick to her stomach to think that he'd actually kissed her and felt sorry about it. She really must be a little *kinder* if she thought she had any chance of winning his heart. After that night, she was sure he would never ask her to go fishing again, and he certainly wouldn't be inviting her to take another ride in his courting buggy.

Silas had tried talking with Rachel on several occasions, but she kept putting him off, saying she was too busy helping his mother. Rachel knew her time of avoidance was almost over, for today's preaching service was being held at their home, and Silas and his family had already arrived.

Rachel was amazed at how quickly the three-hour service went by. Usually it seemed to take forever, but today was different. Maybe it was because Silas was sitting across the aisle and kept sending glances her way. Beyond the flicker of a smile, she had no idea what he was thinking. Was it the kiss they'd shared two weeks ago? Was he waiting for church to be over so he could corner Rachel and tell her he didn't want to see her anymore? If she kept busy in the kitchen, maybe she could avoid him again today. That's just what she planned to do. . .stay busy and out of sight.

Things went well for a while, but tables had been set up out in the barn for eating, and shortly after the noon meal was served, Rachel went back to the house. She planned to get another pot of coffee for the menfolk and carry out one of the pies she and Mom had baked the day before.

Much to Rachel's surprise, she discovered Silas leaning against the cupboard, arms folded across his chest, a silly grin plastered on his face. "I was hopin' you'd come to the kitchen," he said, taking a few steps in her direction.

She made no reply, but moved quickly toward the stove and grabbed the pot of coffee.

"How's about goin' for a walk with me, so we can talk?"

he asked, following her across the room.

Rachel averted her gaze and headed for the door, forgetting about the apple pie she was planning to take back to the barn. "As you can probably see, I'm kinda busy right now," she mumbled.

"You won't be helpin' serve all day," he reminded. "How about after you're done?"

"I really don't think we have anything to talk about."

Silas stepped in front of her, blocking the door. "Please, Rachel. . .just for a few minutes? I've wanted to talk to you for the last two weeks, but there never seemed to be a good time." He smiled. "Besides, I had some stuff to pray about."

Rachel nodded slowly. *"Jah,* me, too."

"So, can we meet out by the willow tree, say in one hour?"

She shrugged. "Okay."

❧

At the appointed time, Rachel donned a heavy sweater and stepped onto the front porch. The afternoon air had cooled considerably, and a chill shivered through her. She caught sight of Silas out in the yard, talking to one of his cousins. She started across the lawn, but stopped just before she reached the weeping willow tree. Silas was saying something to Rudy, and her ears perked up. She was sure he had mentioned her sister's name. *Why would Silas be talking to his cousin about Anna?*

A group of *kinder* ran past, laughing and hollering so loud she couldn't make out what either Silas or Rudy were saying anymore.

David Yoder, a child with Down's syndrome, waved to Rachel, and she waved back, hoping he wouldn't call out her name. The last thing she needed was for Silas to catch her listening in on his conversation.

The children finally wandered off, and Rachel breathed a sigh of relief. She leaned heavily against the trunk of the tree and turned her attention back to Silas and his cousin.

"So, you're in love with her?" she heard Rudy ask.

"Afraid so," Silas answered. "Don't rightly think I'll ever find anyone else I could love as much."

Rachel's heart slammed into her chest. Even after all these months, Silas still wasn't over Anna. *That's probably why he said he was sorry for kissin' me,* she fumed. *Most likely, he was wishin' it had been Anna and not me in his courtin' buggy.*

Tears burned the back of Rachel's eyes. She should have known better than to allow her emotions to get carried away. Silas cared nothing about her, and he never had. He still loved Anna and probably always would, even though she was married and had left the Amish faith. She knew many people carried a torch for lost loves, and because of their pain, they never found love again. Mom had told her once that it almost happened to her great-aunt Mim. She was jilted by her first love, and for many years she carried a torch for him. Finally, she set her feelings aside and learned to love again. But that was only because she'd allowed the Lord to work on her bitter spirit. Rachel wasn't so sure Silas wanted to find love again—especially with a *kinder* like her.

Tired of trying to analyze things, Rachel spun around. She was about to head back to the house, when she felt someone's hand touch her shoulder. "Where ya headin'? I thought we were goin' for a walk."

Rachel shrugged Silas's hand away. "I heard ya talkin' to Rudy. If you're still pinin' for Anna, then why bother takin' a walk with a little *kinder* like me?"

Rudy raised his eyebrows and moved away, but Silas kept walking beside her. When she didn't slow down, he grabbed her around the waist and pulled her to his side. "We need to talk."

Like a tightly-coiled spring, Rachel released her fury on him. "Let go of me!" Her eyes were burning like fire, and she almost choked on the knot lodged in her throat.

"Was ist letz?"

"Nothin's wrong!" she shouted.

Silas opened his mouth as if to say something more, but she cut him off. "Save it! I've heard all I need to know." She darted away without even a backward glance. She'd been a fool to think she could ever make Silas forget about Anna and fall in love with her. She'd been stupid to get caught up in a dumb thing like this. . .letting herself hope the impossible. The one thing she'd enjoyed most about her friendship with Silas was how comfortable they seemed with each other. Not anymore, though. That all ended when she'd heard him tell Rudy that he was still in love with Anna. If Silas wanted to pine his life away for a love he'd never have, then that was *his* problem. Rachel planned to get on with her life!

‌⁂

Silas groaned as he watched Rachel race up the steps and disappear into her house. One of the Beachys' dogs howled, and the mournful sound echoed in his soul. Rachel had heard something he'd told Rudy, but she refused to let him explain. Now everything was ruined between them, and it was a bitter pill to swallow. There was no chance of a relationship with Rachel Beachy because she didn't trust him. Maybe with good reason. He hadn't been so good at trusting lately, either. He'd said he never wanted to move away from God, but he felt himself slipping into despair.

He turned toward his horse and buggy. There was no point in hanging around here. Maybe he should accept things as they were and get on with his life.

fifteen

Rachel felt such relief when Katie Swartley's cast finally came off and she was able to stay home, even if it did mean spending more time helping Pauline in the greenhouse. Anything would be better than facing Silas every day. Knowing he was still in love with Anna and unable to quit loving him herself, Rachel felt a sense of hopelessness. Everything looked different now—the trees weren't as green, the birdsong wasn't as bright. She had nothing to praise God for anymore, and her times of prayer and Bible study became less and less.

The next singing was planned for the second Sunday in November and was to be held at the Hostetlers' place. Joseph had already made it clear that he would be going, and it was obvious that he and Pauline were officially courting. Even though Rachel was happy for them, she couldn't help but feel sorry for herself.

"Are you goin' to the singin' tonight?" her brother asked as they met in the barn that morning before church.

She shook her head. "I don't think so."

"Why not? It could be the last one for awhile, now that the weather's turnin' colder."

She shrugged. "I plan to work on my hope chest tonight."

Joseph grabbed her arm as she started to walk away. "It's Silas Swartley, ain't it? You haven't been actin' right for the last few weeks, and I have a hunch it's got somethin' to do with your feelin's for him."

Rachel felt a familiar burning at the back of her eyes, and she blinked rapidly, hoping to keep the tears from falling. "I'd rather not talk about Silas, if ya don't mind." She shrugged her arm away. "I need to feed the kittens, and if I'm not mistaken, you've got a few chores to do as well."

Joseph moved into the horse's stall without another word, and Rachel let out a sigh of relief. She and Joseph might not always see eye-to-eye, but at least he cared enough about her feelings to drop the subject of Silas Swartley.

As Rachel rounded the corner of the barn, she noticed Dad, down on his knees beside the woodpile. His face was screwed up in obvious pain, and his deep moan confirmed that fact. Rachel rushed to his side and squatted beside him. "*Was ist letz?* You look like you're hurtin' real bad."

"I strained my back tryin' to lift a big hunk of wood. Must've bent over wrong." Dad groaned. "Don't think I can get up on my own, Rachel. Can ya go get Joseph?"

Rachel gently patted her father's shoulder. "*Jah,* sure. Just hang on a few more minutes and try to relax." She jumped up and bolted for the barn.

Joseph was still feeding the horses, and she hurried into the stall where he was forking hay. "*Mach schnell*—go quickly! Dad needs your help."

Joseph lifted his brows in question. "I'm busy, Rachel. Can't he get Perry to do whatever needs doin'?"

Rachel clutched his arm as he was about to jab the pitchfork into another bale of hay. "Dad's hurt his back and can't even stand up. Perry ain't strong enough to get him on his feet, much less help him into the house."

Joseph's blue eyes widened, and he dropped the pitchfork immediately. "Where is he?"

"Out by the woodpile."

Joseph raced from the barn, and Rachel was right behind him. They found their father in the same position as he'd been in when Rachel left him, only now, little beads of sweat covered his forehead. Rachel knew he must be hurting something awful, and she felt deep compassion for him.

Joseph grabbed Dad under one arm, and Rachel took hold of the other one. "On the count of three," Joseph instructed. "One. . .two. . .three!"

Dad moaned as they pulled him to his feet. Walking slightly bent over, he allowed Joseph and Rachel to support most of his weight as they slowly made their way to the house.

They found Mom in the kitchen, sitting in her wheelchair at the table, drinking a cup of tea. Elizabeth and Perry sat across from her, finishing up their bowls of oatmeal.

"Ach, my!" Mom cried. "What's wrong, Daniel? It appears you can barely walk."

Dad grunted and placed his hands on the edge of the cupboard for support. "Fool back went out on me, Rebekah. Happened when I was gettin' more wood." He swallowed real hard, like he was having a hard time talking. "Guess I'll have to make a trip to town tomorrow and see Doc Landers for some poppin' and crackin'. He'll have me back on my feet in no time a'tall."

Rachel glanced over at Joseph, and he gave her a knowing look. The last time Dad's back went out, it took more than a few days' rest or a couple of treatments with the chiropractor to get him back on his feet. There was no doubt about it, Dad wouldn't be going to church this morning, and more than likely he'd be flat on his back in bed for the next several weeks.

❧

Silas had just arrived at the singing, and he was hoping to find Rachel there as well. She'd seemed so distant lately—nothing like the fun-loving Rachel he'd gone fishing with a few weeks ago. Maybe he'd have a chance to clear things up with her. Even if there was no possibility for a future with Rachel, they had a lot in common, and he would still like to be her friend. He remembered how much fun they'd had fishing and studying birds, and his heart skipped a beat at the thought of their first kiss.

Silas caught sight of Joseph sitting on one side of the Hostetlers' barn. He was sharing a bale of straw with Pauline, which was no surprise to Silas. He hurried over and squatted down beside them. "Did Rachel come with you tonight? I haven't seen any sign of her."

Joseph shook his head. "She stayed home. Said somethin' about workin' on her hope chest."

"Hmm. . ." was all Silas could manage.

"Besides, our *daed* hurt his back this mornin', and Rachel probably figured Mom would be needin' her."

Silas wrinkled his forehead. "Sorry to hear that. Will he be able to help you finish the harvest?"

"I doubt it. He's in a lot of pain—could barely make it up the stairs and into bed," Joseph answered. "Guess that means Perry will have to stay home from school and help out. I sure can't put the hay up by myself."

Silas shook his head. "No, I guess not." He thought he should say more, but Joseph had turned his attentions to Pauline, so Silas let his thoughts shift back to Rachel.

Wonder why she would be workin' on her hope chest? After the way she acted the other night, it was fairly obvious she was done with me. Sure as anythin', Rachel isn't stocking her hope chest with the idea of marryin' me.

Suddenly, a light seemed to dawn. *Unless she and Abe Lapp are more serious about each other than I realized.* He groaned softly and stood up. Maybe it was for the best. Rachel would probably be better off with Abe anyway. They were closer in age, and Abe hadn't said or done anything to make Rachel mistrust him.

Silas looked down at Joseph and Pauline. "Well, guess I'll head over to the refreshment table and see what's good to eat."

"*Jah,* okay," Joseph muttered, although Silas was pretty sure Rachel's brother hadn't heard a word he'd said. He was too busy flirting with his date.

❧

When Rachel finished helping Mom and Elizabeth clear away and wash the supper dishes, she excused herself to go to her room.

"You're not sleepy already, are ya?" Mom asked, rolling her wheelchair across the kitchen to where Rachel stood by the hallway door. "Since your *daed*'s in bed and Perry's upstairs readin' to him, I thought maybe we three women could work on a puzzle or play a game."

Elizabeth jumped up and down. "Yes! Yes! And let's make a big batch of popcorn!"

Rachel felt terrible about throwing cold water on their plans, but she had work to do upstairs. Besides, she wasn't fit company for anyone tonight. "Maybe some other time," she said apologetically. "I had planned to work on my hope chest tonight."

Mom's eyes brightened. "I'm right glad to hear that, Rachel. I was beginnin' to wonder if you were ever gonna take an interest in marriage or that hope chest your *daed* made for your sixteenth birthday."

I've got an interest, all right. Trouble is, the man I want is in love with my married sister. Rachel sure couldn't tell Mom what she was thinking. She knew that even though her mother rarely spoke of Anna anymore, she still missed her firstborn and was terribly hurt by her decision to go "fancy." There was no point in bringing up a sore subject, so Rachel smiled and said, "See you two in the mornin'."

When Rachel got to her room, she quickly knelt on the floor in front of her hope chest. The last time she'd opened it, she had been filled with such high hopes. Back then she and Silas seemed to be getting closer, and she'd even allowed herself to believe he might actually be falling in love with her. For a brief time she'd been praising God like crazy. Her hopeful dream had been dented when Silas said he was sorry for kissing her, and it had been smashed to smithereens when she'd overheard him telling his cousin Rudy that he still loved Anna. "What's the use in havin' a hope chest if you aren't plannin' to get married?" she murmured. "I could never marry anyone but Silas, because he's the only man I'll ever love."

Rachel lifted the lid and studied the contents of her cedar chest. There was the lamp Dad had given her, along with the pillowcases Mom had made. She'd purchased a few new items as well—a set of dishes, some towels, and a tablecloth. She'd also made a braided throw rug, some pot holders, and had even been thinking about starting a quilt with the double ring pattern. There was no point in making one now. In fact, the best thing to do was either sell off or give away most of the things in her hope chest. She pulled out the set of pillowcases and the braided throw rug, knowing she could use them in her room. The other things she put in a cardboard box, planning to take them to the greenhouse the following day.

Since Christmas wasn't far off, she was fairly certain she could sell some things to their customers. Anything that didn't sell, she would take to Thomas Benner, the owner of The Country Store in Paradise, and see if he might put them out on consignment. Maybe she would use the money she made to buy a concrete birdbath for Mom's flower garden. If she got enough from the sales, she might also buy several bird feeders from Eli Yoder, which would bring even more birds into their yard. At least she could still take some pleasure in bird-watching—even though it would have to be without Silas Swartley. As long as she was able to get away by herself to enjoy the great outdoors, Rachel could endure anything—even losing Silas to the memory of her sister.

Rachel's only concern was what her mother would think when she saw her things for sale in the greenhouse. Mom had seemed so hopeful about Rachel adding items to her hope chest. If she knew what was really going on, she'd probably get all nervous, thinking she'd have to wait until Elizabeth grew up before she could plan a wedding. Of course, if things kept on the way they were with Joseph and Pauline, Mom could be in on their wedding plans.

Rachel closed the empty chest, and in doing so, she spotted Anna's hope chest. All these months it had been in the corner of her room, and never once had she opened it. It was all she had left of her sister. If she opened it now, memories of Anna and reminders of how much she missed her would probably make her cry. She already felt enough pain and didn't think she could bear any more right now.

Rachel ran her fingers along the top of Anna's cedar chest as tears slipped from her eyes and rolled down her cheeks. "Oh, Anna, wasn't it bad enough that you broke Silas's heart by marryin' his best friend? Did ya really have to move away and go English on us?" Rachel choked on a sob as she turned away from Anna's hope chest. *Will I ever see Anna again? Will I ever marry and become a mama?*

sixteen

Silas tossed and turned most of the night. He had to see Rachel again and try to explain things. Even if she never wanted to court him, he needed to clear the air and make her understand the way he was feeling. If only they could spend more time together. As he drifted off to sleep, visions of Rachel's sweet face and two little dimples filled up his senses. If only. . .

When Silas awoke the next morning, he had a plan. Rachel had been kind enough to help out at their place when Mom broke her arm, so now he could return the favor. If he helped Joseph get in the hay, he'd be busy out in the fields most of the day, but mealtimes would be spent in the Beachys' kitchen. It would be a good chance to see Rachel and maybe get in a word or two with her. It was worth a try. Besides, Daniel Beachy was laid up right now. He was sure the man would welcome his help.

❧

Rachel had just finished washing and drying the breakfast dishes when she heard a horse and buggy pull into the yard. She peeked out the kitchen window and gulped when she saw who it was. Silas Swartley had climbed out of his buggy and was heading toward the house.

Joseph and Perry were in the fields. Elizabeth was at school. Dad and Mom had gone into town to see Doc Landers. That left Rachel all alone at the house. Silas had seen her through the window and waved. She had no other choice but to open the door.

"Gut Morgen," Silas said when Rachel answered his knock. "I missed you at the singin' last night."

"I had other things to do," she replied stiffly.

"So I heard." Silas's forehead wrinkled. "I also heard your *daed* hurt his back."

Rachel nodded. "It goes out on him now and then. He's at the chiropractor's right now." She still hadn't invited Silas inside, and since she didn't plan to, Rachel stepped out onto the porch, hoping he would take the hint and be on his way.

"I came to help with the harvest," Silas surprised her by saying. "Joseph said your *daed* won't be up to it now, and since we're all done harvestin' over at our place, I figured I'd offer my services here."

Rachel flicked an imaginary piece of lint off the sleeve of her dress and tried to avoid his steady gaze. "That's right nice of you," she murmured. "Perry stayed home from school to help Joseph today. But it won't be good if he misses too many days."

"That's what I thought." Silas shifted from one foot to the other. "I—uh—was kinda hopin' you and I could have a little talk before I head on out to the fields."

Rachel blinked. "There ain't nothin' to talk about. Besides, I've gotta get to the greenhouse and open up."

"I thought Pauline worked in the greenhouse."

"She does, but she's got chores at her house to do every mornin', so she usually doesn't get here 'til ten or after."

Silas cleared his throat. "Okay, I'll let ya get to it then." He pivoted and started down the steps, but when he got to the bottom, he halted and turned back around. "Maybe later we can talk?"

She raised her gaze to his and nodded slowly. *"Jah,* maybe."

❧

Silas saw tears clinging like dewdrops to Rachel's long, pale lashes. It was all he could do to keep from pulling her into his arms. Before their misunderstanding, he'd been drawing closer to Rachel, and some of his old fears had been sliding into a locked trunk of unwanted memories. Now he wondered why they had drifted apart. Maybe the real issue was trust. Did she trust him? Did he trust her?

A deep sense of longing inched its way through Silas's body. He'd missed seeing Rachel every day, and if the look on her sweet face was any indication of the way she felt, then he was fairly certain she'd been missing him, too.

"See you later, Rachel." Silas offered her his best smile, lifted a hand to wave, then headed for the fields.

"Later," she mumbled.

⁂

Rachel entered the greenhouse, carrying her box of hope chest items in her arms and a lot of confusion in her brain. It was kind of Silas to offer his help with the hay harvest, but how would she handle him coming over every day? She'd tried so hard to get him out of her mind, and now him wanting to talk had her real concerned. Was he planning to tell her again how sorry he was for that unexpected kiss of a few weeks ago? Did he want to explain why he still loved Anna, even though they could never be together? Well, Rachel already knew that much, and she sure as anything didn't need to hear it again. She'd made up her mind—she was not going to say anything more to Silas than a polite word or two—no matter how many days he came to help out. Somehow she must keep her feelings under control.

Rachel shivered as goose bumps erupted on her arms, and she knew it wasn't from the chill in the greenhouse. "Get busy," she scolded herself. "It's the only thing that will keep you sane."

Rachel quickly set to work pricing her hope chest items, then she placed them on an empty shelf near the front door. She had no more than put the OPEN sign in the window, when the first customer of the day showed up. It was Laura Yoder, and Rachel breathed a sigh of relief when she saw that the pretty redhead was alone. The last time Laura came to the greenhouse, she'd brought both of her children along.

Barbara, who was two and a half, had pulled one of Mom's prized African violets off the shelf, and the little girl had quite a time playing in all that rich, black dirt. Laura's four-year-old son, David, had been so full of questions. The child's handicap didn't slow him down much, and, like most children his age, David was curious about everything.

As much as Rachel loved *kinder,* it sorely tried her patience when they came in with their folks and ran about the greenhouse like it was a play yard. If it was disturbing to her, she could only imagine how her other customers might feel. Most Amish parents were quite strict and didn't let their children get away with much, but Laura seemed to be more tolerant of her children's antics. However, Rachel was pretty sure she would step in and discipline, should it become absolutely necessary.

"I see you're all alone today," Rachel said as her customer began to look around the store.

Laura nodded. "I left the little ones with Eli's *mamm.* I've got several errands to run, and I figured I could get them done much quicker if I was by myself." She chuckled. "Besides, Mary Ellen seems to like her role as Grandma."

Rachel smiled. "I guess she would. Let's see. . .how many grandchildren does she have now?"

"Five in all. Martha Rose has three, as I'm sure you know. And of course, there's my two busy little ones. Mary Ellen's son, Lewis, and his wife are expectin' most any day, so soon there'll be six." Laura moved over by the shelf where Rachel had displayed her hope chest items. "There's some right nice things here. If I didn't already have a sturdy set of dishes, I'd be tempted to buy these," she said, fingering the edge of a white stoneware cup.

"Guess the right buyer will come along sooner or later," Rachel remarked, making no reference to the fact that they were her hope chest dishes. Mom hadn't been very happy when she learned that Rachel was bringing them here, but Rachel was relieved when she chose not to make an issue of it. Truth be told, her mother was probably praying that Rachel's things wouldn't sell and some nice fellow would come along and propose marriage real soon.

"How's the flower business?" Laura asked, pulling Rachel out of her reflections.

"Oh, fair to middlin'," she replied with a nod. Rachel didn't feel the inclination to tell Laura that except for the need to help out, she really didn't care much about the flower business. Laura Yoder seemed like such a prim and proper sort of lady. She probably wouldn't understand Rachel's desire to be outdoors, enjoying all the wildlife God had created.

Sometimes Rachel wished she'd been born a boy, just so she could spend more time outside. Even baling or bucking hay would be preferable to being cooped up inside a stuffy old greenhouse all day.

"Have you got any yellow mums?" Laura asked, once more breaking into Rachel's thoughts.

"Mums? Oh, sure, I think we've got several colors," Rachel answered with a nod. "Come with me to the other room and we'll see what's available."

Rachel studied Laura as she checked over the chrysanthemums. Even though her hair was red and her face was pretty, she looked plain, just like all other Amish women. It was hard to imagine that she was ever part of the fancy, English world. Rachel had been a girl when Eli Yoder married Laura, and she'd only met her after Laura had chosen to become Amish. She had no idea how Laura used to look dressed in modern clothes or even how the woman felt about her past life. *Maybe I should ask her a few questions about bein' English. It might help me better understand why Anna left home.*

Taking a deep breath for courage, Rachel plunged ahead. "Say, Laura, I was wonderin' about somethin'."

Laura picked up a yellow mum plant and pivoted to face Rachel. "What is it?"

"I know you used to be English."

Laura nodded.

"You've probably heard that my sister Anna married Reuben Yutzy awhile back, and the two of them left the faith and moved to Lancaster."

Laura's expression turned solemn. *"Jah,* I know about that."

"Except for one letter Anna sent to your sister-in-law, Martha Rose, we haven't heard a word from her," Rachel said with a catch in her voice. "It sure hurts knowin' she's no longer part of our family."

Laura gently touched Rachel's shoulder. "I'm sure it's not easy for any of you. . .not even Anna."

Rachel's eyes filled with unexpected tears, and she sniffed. "Ya really think it pains her, too?"

"I'm almost certain of it." Laura drew in a deep breath and let it out with a soft moan. "It hurt my folks when I left the English world to become Amish. They never quit lovin' me or offerin' their support, though. We stayed in touch, and pretty soon my *daed* surprised me real good by sellin' his law practice and movin' out to a small farm nearby." She smiled. "My folks are still English, of course, but they're livin' a much simpler life now, and me and the *kinder* get to see lots more of them."

"Do you think there's a chance that Anna and my folks will ever mend their fences—even if Anna and Reuben never reconcile with the church? Maybe even come to the point where they can start visitin' each other from time to time?"

Laura clasped Rachel's hand. "I'll surely pray for that, as I'm sure you're already doin'."

"Jah, that and a whole lot of other things."

Laura followed Rachel back to the front of the greenhouse, where she wrapped a strip of brown paper around the plant and wrote up a bill. Laura paid her, picked up the mum, and was just about to open the front door when Pauline came rushing in. Her cheeks were pink, and a few strands of tawny yellow hair peeked out from under her *Kapp.* "Whew! It's gettin' a bit windy out there!" she exclaimed.

Laura laughed. "I can tell. You look like you've been standin' underneath a windmill, for goodness' sake."

Pauline giggled and reached up to readjust her covering, which was slightly askew. "Sure is a *gut* day to be indoors. I'm mighty glad I have this job workin' at Grandma's Place."

Wish I could say the same, Rachel thought ruefully. *"For I have learned, in whatsoever state I am, therewith to be content."* The verse from Philippians that Mom often liked to quote came popping into Rachel's mind. *Okay, Lord, I'll try harder.*

Pauline asked about Laura's *kinder,* and Laura spent the next few minutes telling her how much they were growing. She even told how her cat, Foosie, had paired up with one of the barn cats. Now the children had a bunch of fluffy brown-and-white kittens to occupy their busy little hands.

It amazed Rachel the way the two women visited, as though they'd always been friends. She knew from the talk she'd heard that it wasn't so. Truth be told, Pauline used to dislike Laura because she had stolen Eli Yoder's heart and he'd married her and not Pauline.

Rachel could relate well to the pain of knowing the man you loved was carrying a torch for someone else and didn't see you as anything more than a friend. She couldn't imagine how Pauline had gotten through those difficult years after Eli had jilted her and married an English woman. It amazed her to see that there was no animosity between the two women now.

Laura finally headed out, and Pauline got right to work watering plants and repotting some that had outgrown their containers. She was so happy doing her work that she was actually humming.

"Say, I was wonderin' if you'd mind me askin' a personal question," Rachel asked when Pauline finally took a break and sat down on the stool behind the cash register.

"Sure, what is it?"

Rachel leaned on the other side of the counter and offered Pauline a brief smile. She hoped her question wasn't out of line and wouldn't be taken the wrong way. "I know you and Laura were at odds for a while, and I was wonderin' what happened to make you so friendly with one another."

Pauline smiled. "I used to be jealous of Laura because I felt she stole Eli away from me. After she had David and went home to her folks, I was even hopin' Eli and I might still have a chance. But then she came back to Lancaster Valley, and when she did, she was like a changed person. She'd found Jesus, and one day she came callin' on me. Said we needed to have a little talk."

Rachel's interest was definitely piqued. "Really? Mind if I ask what was said?"

Pauline shrugged. "Nothin' much except Laura apologized for making me so miserable, and I told her I was sorry, too." She frowned deeply. "The thing was, I knew in my heart that Eli had never been in love with me. He and I were only *gut* friends. From the very beginning, I should have been Christian enough to turn loose of him and let him find the kind of happiness with Laura that he deserved. Truth be told, Eli probably did me a favor by marryin' Laura."

Rachel's eyebrows shot up. "Really? How's that?"

Pauline smiled. "If he'd married me, I never would have gotten to know Joe so well, and we. . ." Her words trailed off, and she blushed a deep crimson. "Guess you've probably figured out that I'm in love with your big brother."

Rachel grinned back at Pauline. *"Jah,* and I'm positive he feels the selfsame way about you." She turned and glanced across the room at her hope chest items. "Say, ya think ya might be interested in some things for your hope chest?"

seventeen

Daniel Beachy's back took nearly two weeks to heal, and Silas came over every day but Sunday to help with chores and the last of the harvesting. In all that time, he never had his heart-to-heart talk with Rachel. It wasn't because he hadn't tried. He'd made every effort to get her alone, but she always made up some excuse about being too busy. Silas was getting discouraged and had about decided to give up when he devised a plan. Yesterday had been his last day helping out. Daniel had assured him that he was feeling well enough to start doing some light chores, and the hay had been baled and put away in the barn. Silas wouldn't be going back to the Beachy farm—at least not to help out. However, that didn't mean he couldn't pay a little visit to the greenhouse.

❧

Since none of Rachel's hope chest items had sold yet, she decided it might be time to take them into town and see if Thomas Benner would sell them in his store. There had been storm clouds brewing that morning, and Dad wouldn't let Rachel take the horse and buggy to town because he was worried she might get caught in a snowstorm. She'd really been hoping to get her things into The Country Store in time for the busy Christmas shopping season. Now she'd have to wait until the weather improved. Besides, Mom had come down with a cold, and it wouldn't be fair to expect her to work with Pauline in the greenhouse while Rachel went to town.

Rachel donned her woolen cape and headed for the greenhouse. She'd talked her mother into going back to bed and had left a warm pot of fenugreek tea by her bedside. Mom would be resting, and Rachel would be all by herself until Pauline showed up. If the weather got real bad, Pauline might not come today. For that matter, they may not even have any customers. Who in their right mind would want to visit a greenhouse when the weather was cold and threatening to snow?

Shortly after she opened the greenhouse and stoked up the wood-burning stove, Rachel heard a horse and buggy pull up. Figuring it was probably Pauline, she flung open the door. To her astonishment, Abe Lapp stepped down from his closed-in buggy. She hadn't seen Abe since the last preaching service, and then she'd only spoken a few words to him when she was serving the menfolk.

"Looks like it could storm," Abe said when he entered the greenhouse. He was wearing a dark wool jacket, and his black felt hat was pulled down over his ears.

Ears that are a might too big, Rachel noticed. An image of Silas sifted through her mind. *Abe's not nearly as good-looking as Silas, but then—as Dad often says—looks ain't everythin'.*

"What can I help you with, Abe?" Rachel asked as she slipped behind the counter and took a seat on her stool.

Abe took off his hat, and it was all Rachel could do to keep from laughing out loud. A bunch of his hair stood straight up. It looked as though he hadn't bothered to comb it that morning.

"I really didn't come here to buy anything," Abe said, looking kind of embarrassed. He jammed his free hand inside his coat pocket and offered her a crooked grin.

"What did ya come for?"

"I—uh—was wonderin' if you'd like to go to the next singin' with me."

Rachel frowned. "There's gonna be another one? I thought with the weather turnin' bad and all, there would be no more singin's 'til spring."

Abe shrugged. "There's supposed to be one this Sunday night, out at Herman Weaver's place. Guess if the weather gets real nasty, they'll have to cancel it."

Rachel wasn't sure what to say next. She didn't want to go to any singing—with or without Abe Lapp. She'd known Abe and his family a good many years and knew Abe was a nice enough fellow. He just wasn't Silas Swartley, and if she couldn't be courted by the man she loved, she didn't want to be courted at all. *Of course, you could just go as friends,* a little voice reminded. Still, that might lead Abe on, and she didn't want him to start thinking there was any chance for the two of them as a couple.

"So, what's your answer?" Abe asked, breaking into Rachel's disconcerting thoughts. "Can I come by your place Sunday night and give you a lift to the Weavers'?"

Rachel chewed on her lower lip as she searched for the right words. She didn't want to hurt Abe's feelings, but her answer had to be no. "I'm flattered that you'd want to escort me to the singin', but I'm afraid I can't go."

Abe's dark eyebrows drew downward. "Can't, or won't?"

She swallowed hard. "My *mamm* has a bad cold, and Dad just got on his feet after a bout with his back. I think it's best for me to stick close to home."

Abe nodded and slapped his hat back on his head. "Good enough. I'll see you around then." With that, he marched out the door.

Rachel followed, hoping to call out a friendly good-bye, but Abe was already in his buggy and had taken up the reins. *Maybe I made a mistake,* she lamented. *Maybe I should have agreed to go with him. Wouldn't Abe be better than no one?*

She bowed her head and prayed, "Lord, if I'm not supposed to love Silas, please give me the grace to accept it."

As if on cue, she noticed there was another buggy parked in the driveway, and she recognized the driver. Rachel's heart started hammering real hard, and her hands felt like a couple of slippery trout as she watched Silas Swartley step down from his buggy and start walking toward the greenhouse. She couldn't imagine why he would be here. The harvest was done, and Dad's back was much better.

Silas rubbed his hands briskly together as he entered the greenhouse. His nose was red from the cold, and his black felt hat was covered with tiny snowflakes. Dad had been right. . .the snow was here.

Rachel moved over to the counter, her heart riding on the waves of expectation. Silas followed. "It's mighty cold out. Guess winter's decided to come a bit early." He nodded toward the door. "Say, wasn't that Abe Lapp I saw gettin' into his buggy?"

"*Jah,* it was Abe."

"Did he buy out the store?"

She shook her head. "Nope, didn't buy a thing."

Silas raised his eyebrows. "How come?"

"Abe stopped by to ask me to the singin' this Sunday night," Rachel said with a shrug. "Can I help ya with somethin', Silas?"

He squinted his dark eyes, and Rachel wondered why he made no comment about Abe's invitation.

"I came by to see if you have any poinsettias. Mom's sister lives in Ohio, and she's comin' to visit soon. She thought since her birthday's soon, she'd give her a plant," Silas mumbled.

Rachel stepped out from behind the counter. "I believe we still have one or two poinsettias in the other room. Shall we go take a look-see?"

Silas followed silently as they went to the room where a variety of plants were on display. Rachel showed him several poinsettias, and he selected the largest one.

Back at the manually-operated cash register, Rachel noticed her hands were trembling as she counted out Silas's change. Just the nearness of him took her breath away, and it irked her to think he had the power to make her feel so weak in the knees.

"Seen any interestin' birds lately?" Silas asked when she handed him the plant.

Glad for the diversion, she smiled. "I saw a great horned owl the other night when I was lookin' up in the tree with my binoculars. The critter was sure hootin' like crazy."

Silas chuckled, then he started for the door. Just as he got to the shelf where Rachel's hope chest items were placed, he stopped and bent down to examine them. "These look like some mighty fine dishes. Mind if I ask how much they cost?"

"The price sticker is on the bottom of the top plate," she answered.

Silas picked it up and whistled. "Kind of high, don'tcha think?" His face turned redder than the plant he was holding. "Sorry. Guess it's not my place to decide how much your folks should be sellin' things for."

Rachel thought about telling him that it wasn't Mom or Dad who'd priced the dishes, but she didn't want Silas to know she was selling off her hope chest items. She forced a smile and said, "I hope your aunt enjoys the poinsettia."

Silas nodded and opened the front door. "I hope Abe Lapp knows how lucky he is," he called over his shoulder.

Rachel slowly shook her head. "Now what in the world did he mean by that? Surely Silas doesn't think me and Abe are courtin'." Of course, she hadn't bothered to tell him that she'd turned down Abe's offer to escort her to the singing. But then, he hadn't asked, either.

Rachel moved over to the window and watched with a heavy heart as Silas drove out of sight. She glanced over at the dishes he'd said were too high-priced and wondered if he had considered buying them, maybe as a gift for his mother or aunt.

"Guess I should lower the price some." Rachel felt moisture on her cheeks. She'd been trying so hard to be hopeful and keep praising God, but after seeing Silas again, she realized her hopes had been for nothing. He obviously had no interest in her. Rachel wondered if God even cared about her. Hadn't He been listening to her prayers and praises all these months? Didn't He realize how much her heart ached for Silas Swartley?

eighteen

It snowed hard for the next few days, but on Saturday the weather improved some, so Rachel convinced Joseph to hitch up the sleigh and drive her to The Country Store. It was only the second week of December, but there was still a chance people would be looking for things to give as Christmas presents. She had finally sold some towels and a few pot holders to customers at the greenhouse, but she still needed to get rid of the dishes, the kerosene lamp, and a tablecloth.

Thomas Benner was more than happy to take Rachel's things on consignment, although he did mention that they would have had a better chance of selling if she'd brought them in a few weeks earlier.

By the time Rachel left the store and found Joseph, who'd gone looking for something to give Pauline for Christmas, it was beginning to snow again.

"We'd best be gettin' on home," Joseph said, looking up at the sky. "If this keeps on, the roads could get mighty slippery. I wouldn't want some car to go slidin' into our sleigh."

"You're right, we should leave now," Rachel said as she climbed into the sleigh. She reached under the seat and withdrew an old quilt, wrapping it snugly around the lower half of her body. "Brr. . .it's gettin' downright cold!"

Joseph picked up the reins and got the horse moving. "Yep, sure is."

Rachel glanced over at her brother. He seemed to be off in some other world. "So, what'd you get for Pauline?"

He smiled. "I bought her a pair of gardening gloves and a book about flowers."

"She should like that, since she enjoys working in the green-house so much."

Joseph nodded. "She's sure changed, don'tcha think?"

Rachel bit back the laughter bubbling in her throat. "I think you've been *gut* for her."

His dark eyebrows lifted. "You really think so?"

"I do."

"Well, she's been *gut* for me, too."

"She's not worried about your age difference anymore?"

He shook his head. "Nope, doesn't seem to be."

"And you're okay with it?"

"Yep."

"I'm glad."

"Come spring, I'm thinkin' about askin' her to marry me." Joseph glanced over at Rachel. "Don't you goin' sayin' anything now, ya hear?"

"Oh, I won't," she assured him. "It's not my place to tell."

"I'm sorry things didn't work out for you and Silas," Joseph said sincerely.

Rachel grimaced. "It wasn't meant to be, that's all. I just have to learn to be content with my life as it is. There's no point in hopin' for the impossible. Job in the Bible did, and look where it got him."

"Think about it, Rachel. Even through all his trials, Job never lost hope," Joseph reminded, "and in the end, God blessed Job with even more than he'd lost."

Rachel drew in a deep breath. "I guess you're right, but it's not always easy to have hope. Especially when things don't go as we've planned."

"Life is full of twists and turns," Joseph remarked. "It's how we choose to deal with things that makes the difference in our attitudes. Our hope should be in Jesus, not man, and not on our circumstances."

Rachel stared out the front window. She didn't want to talk

about Job, hope, or even God right now. She was too worried about the weather. The snow was coming down harder, and the road was completely covered. She watched the passing scenery, noting that the yard of the one-room schoolhouse was empty. No bicycles. No scooters. No sign of any children. "School must have been dismissed early today. Nancy Frey probably thought it would be best to let the *kinder* go before the weather got any worse," she commented.

They rode along in silence awhile, until a rescue vehicle came sailing past, its red lights blinking off and on and the siren blaring to beat the band.

"Must be an accident up ahead," Joseph said, pulling back on the reins to slow the horse down.

Rachel felt her body tense. She hated the thought of seeing an accident, and she prayed one of their Amish buggies wasn't involved. So often horse-drawn buggies had been damaged by cars that either didn't see them or had been traveling too fast. Lots of Amish folks had been injured from collisions with those fast-moving automobiles.

Their sleigh had just rounded the next bend when they saw the rescue vehicle in the middle of the road. There were flares along the highway, a car pulled off on the shoulder, and rescue workers bent over a small figure. Several Amish children were clustered around, and a policeman was directing traffic.

"We'd better stop," Joseph said. "It could be someone we know." He pulled the buggy off the road, then he and Rachel jumped out.

They had only taken a few steps when a familiar voice called out, "Joseph! Rachel! Over here!"

Rachel glanced to her right. Elizabeth was running across the slippery snow, and she nearly knocked Rachel off her feet when she grabbed her around the middle. "It's Perry! He was hit by that car!"

The next several hours were like a terrible nightmare for

the Beachy family. Perry had been killed instantly when the car hit a patch of ice and swerved off the road. All the other Amish children who'd been walking home from school had witnessed the accident, and most of them were in shock.

Rachel went through the motions of getting supper on, as Mom and Dad took care of the funeral arrangements and answered all sorts of questions for the authorities. No one could believe that young, impetuous Perry, who'd been making jokes at breakfast that same morning, was dead. He was up in heaven now, with relatives and friends who'd gone on before him. Rachel found some comfort in knowing he was with Jesus, but oh, how she would miss his smiling, often mischievous face. She knew the rest of the family felt the same way—especially Mom, who had lost her youngest child.

Rachel stirred the pot of lentil soup she was making for supper, and her thoughts went instinctively to Anna, whose favorite soup was lentil. *Anna needs to be told about Perry. She's still part of this family, even if she has moved away. She will probably want to come home for the funeral.*

Several women had come to the house with food and offers of help, and one of them was Martha Rose Zook. She'd received a few letters from Anna, so she would be the logical one to ask about getting word to her.

Rachel hurried to the living room just as Martha Rose and Laura Yoder were about to head out. "Wait, Martha Rose!" she called. "I need to speak with you."

Martha Rose moved away from the door, and Rachel motioned her into the kitchen. She didn't want anyone to overhear their conversation, especially not Mom or Dad.

"What is it, Rachel?" Martha Rose asked, offering her a sympathetic look. "Is there somethin' more I can do?"

Rachel nodded, as stinging tears clung to her lashes. "Could ya let Anna know what's happened today? She'll no doubt wanna be here for the funeral. It wouldn't be goin' against the ban to—"

Martha Rose hugged Rachel, interrupting her plea. "Of course I'll let her know. I have her address and phone number, so I'll just go to the nearest pay phone and give her a call."

Rachel smiled through her tears. *"Danki,* I'd sure appreciate that." She glanced toward the door leading to the living room. "Just the same, it might be best if ya didn't say anything to anyone about this."

Martha Rose held up her hand. "I won't say a word."

੨ঌ

The funeral for Perry was two days later, and friends, relatives, and neighbors quickly filled up the Beachy house for the service. A plain pine coffin sat in one corner of the room, displaying young Perry's body, all dressed in white.

It sent shivers up Rachel's back to see her little brother lying there so still and pale. In this life, she would never have the pleasure of seeing him run and play. Never hear his contagious laugh or squeals of delight when a calf or kitten was born. It wasn't fair! She wondered why God allowed so much hurt to come into the world and had to keep reminding herself that even though Perry's days on earth were done, he did have a new life in heaven.

Rachel glanced around the room, noting that Silas and his family were in attendance. Silas caught her looking his way and offered a sympathetic smile. She only nodded in response and gulped back the sob rising in her throat.

Rachel was miserable without Silas as a friend, and now they'd lost another family member. *Anna may as well be dead,* she silently moaned. *She's not one of us anymore, and even though Martha Rose called her on the phone and told her about the funeral, she chose not to come.* Unbidden tears slipped out of Rachel's eyes and rolled down her cheeks in rivulets that stung like fire. *If only things could be different. If only. . .*

Rachel barely heard the words Bishop Weaver spoke. Her thoughts lingered on her selfish sister and how much she'd hurt the family by going English. She'd hurt Silas, too, and because of it, he'd spurned Rachel's love.

The service was nearly over, and the congregation had just begun the closing hymn when Rachel caught a glimpse of her sister coming in the back door. She had to look twice to be sure it really was Anna. Her modern sister was dressed in English clothes—a pair of black trousers and a royal blue slipover sweater. The biggest surprise was Anna's hair. She'd cut it real short, just like she'd threatened to do before she left home.

Anna slipped quietly onto one of the benches near the back of the room, and Rachel noticed that she was all alone. Apparently Reuben hadn't come. He might have had to work today, or maybe he was afraid to face everyone after all he'd done. Worse yet, maybe he and Anna had split up. What would happen if Anna left Reuben and returned to the Amish faith? Would their marriage be annulled by the bishop? Would Silas. . . ?

Rachel jerked her wayward thoughts aside. No point in borrowing trouble. . .at least not until she knew the facts.

When the benediction was pronounced, Rachel stood up. She knew the funeral procession to the cemetery would begin soon, and she wanted a chance to speak with her sister, just in case she didn't plan on staying.

She'd only taken a few steps when she was stopped by Silas. "I'm real sorry about Perry." He paused, his gaze going to the ceiling, then back again. "It just don't seem right, him bein' so young and all."

Rachel numbly stared at him. When Silas said nothing more, she started to move away. To her surprise, Silas grabbed her around the waist and gave her a hug. She held her arms stiffly at her side and waited until he pulled back.

She was sure his display of affection was nothing more than a brotherly hug. Besides, it was too little too late as far as she was concerned. Rachel knew she needed to weed out the yearning she felt for Silas. It would only cause her further pain to keep pining away and hoping for something that never could be.

She bit her bottom lip in order to keep from bursting into tears, then turned away quickly.

nineteen

Rachel caught up with Anna as she was about to leave the house. "Anna, hold up a minute. I wanna talk to ya."

Anna turned to face Rachel, her green eyes filled with tears. "I probably shouldn't have come, but Perry was my baby brother and I just couldn't stay away. Thanks for askin' Martha Rose to get word to me."

"It's only right that you should be here." Rachel nodded toward the door. "Let's go outside so's we can talk."

Once they were on the porch, Rachel led Anna over to the swing and they both sat down.

"Do you think this is a good idea?" Anna asked. "I'm still under the ban. You might be in trouble for talkin' to me."

Rachel shrugged. "Accordin' to Bishop Weaver, there's really no rule sayin' we can't talk to you a'tall. We're just not supposed to eat at the same table or do any kind of business with ya."

"Guess that's true enough." Anna swallowed hard. "Martha Rose said Perry was hit by a car, but she didn't know any of the details. Can ya tell me how this horrible thing happened?"

Rachel drew in a shuddering breath. "Joseph and me were headin' home from town in the sleigh. As we came around the bend near our driveway, we saw the accident. There was a rescue vehicle, a police car, and—" She choked on her next words. "Perry was lyin' in the road, and we were told that he probably died upon impact."

Anna reached for her hand. "The roads were icy, huh?"

Rachel nodded. "I'm sure the driver of the car didn't mean to run off the road and hit Perry. It was just an accident, but still—" She sniffed deeply. "Perry was so young. It don't

156

seem right when a child is killed."

"I know," Anna agreed. "Sometimes it's hard to figure out why God allows bad things to happen to innocent people."

Rachel let go of Anna's hand and reached up to wipe her eyes. "Mom would remind us that the Bible says God is no respecter of persons, and that rain falls on the just, same as it does the unjust."

"How are Mom and Dad?" Anna asked, taking their conversation in another direction. "I only saw them from a distance, and I didn't think it would be wise to try to talk to them right now." She glanced away. "I'm sure they must hate me for leavin' the faith and all."

Rachel shook her head. *"Himmel!* They don't hate ya, Anna. They're disappointed, of course, but you're still their flesh and blood, and if you were to come back, they'd welcome ya with open arms."

Anna flexed her fingers, then formed them into tight balls in her lap. "I won't be comin' back, Rachel. Reuben and me are happy livin' the modern life. He likes his paintin' job, and I'm content to work as a waitress."

So they're not separated. Guess that's somethin' to be grateful for. "You could have done those things and still remained Amish," Rachel reminded.

"I know, but Reuben really needed a truck to get him back and forth to work, not to mention travelin' from job to job." Anna sighed deeply. "Besides, we both felt the *Ordnung* was too restrictive. We enjoy doin' some worldly things, and—"

"Anna, I hope you're not caught up with drinkin' or drugs!"

Anna shook her head. "No, I—"

"Silas told me Reuben had been runnin' with a wild bunch of English fellows before he married you, and Reuben even admitted to gettin' drunk a few times."

"Jah, he does like a few beers now and then. But he don't get drunk anymore," Anna added quickly.

Rachel wasn't sure what else to say. She knew what Bishop

Weaver's concerns about drinking would be. *One drink can lead to another, and pretty soon you can't quit.* That's what he'd have to say.

"How's Silas Swartley these days?" Anna asked, breaking into Rachel's thoughts. "If he told you about Reuben, then I guess the two of you must be gettin' pretty close."

Rachel shifted uneasily. How much should she tell Anna about her relationship with Silas? Would it be best to say nothing, or did Anna have the right to know that Silas was still in love with her?

"Are ya gonna tell me or not?" Anna pried. "I can see by the look on your face that you're in love with him."

Yeah, and he still loves you. Rachel bit back the words and answered, "Silas and I are friends, nothin' more."

"Has he asked you out?"

"We've done a few things together, but there wasn't anythin' to it."

Anna shrugged. "I was kinda hopin' that after I left home, Silas's eyes would be opened and he'd see how good you'd be for him."

Well, he hasn't! Just thinking about Silas's rejection made Rachel feel cranky. Surely he had to know he wasn't going to get Anna back. Why couldn't he be happy with Rachel? *Guess I've reminded myself before that I wouldn't want his love secondhand.*

"You never really said, how's the rest of the family takin' Perry's death?" Anna asked, imposing on Rachel's thoughts one more time.

Rachel felt a fresh set of tears pool in her eyes. "It's been mighty hard—especially for Mom and Elizabeth. Perry was still Mom's little boy, and even though Elizabeth and her twin fought like cats and dogs, I know she still loved him."

Before Anna could reply, Joseph poked his head through the doorway. He shot Anna a look of irritation. "Kinda late, aren't ya?"

"I caught the bus partway here, then walked the rest of the way," Anna explained. "I came in during the closing hymn."

Joseph shrugged his broad shoulders. "Rachel, I came to tell ya that everyone went out the back door and they're climbin' into their buggies. We'll be headin' for the cemetery now."

Rachel stood up, but when Anna didn't join her, she turned back toward the swing. "Aren't ya comin'? You can ride with me and Joseph."

Anna stared down at her clasped hands. "I'm not sure I should. Some folks might see it as an intrusion."

"How could they?" Rachel questioned. "You're part of our family. You have every right to be at Perry's burial."

Anna looked up at Joseph, and Rachel could see that he was mulling things over. He finally nodded. "You're welcome to ride in the buggy with me and Rachel."

Anna stood up, and Rachel reached for her hand. They stepped off the front porch together and followed Joseph around the back of the house.

❧

A horse-drawn hearse led the procession down the narrow country road, with the two Beachy buggies following. Behind them was a long line of Amish carriages, and Silas Swartley's was the last. He felt sick to the pit of his stomach thinking how it would feel to lose one of his younger brothers. Even if they didn't always see eye-to-eye, they were kin, and blood was thicker than water.

At the cemetery everyone climbed out of their buggies and gathered around the hand-dug grave, then Bishop Weaver said a few words.

Silas stood near his own family, directly across from the Beachys. He was surprised to see Anna standing between Rachel and Joseph. On one hand, it made sense that she would be here, since she was part of their family. On the other hand, she'd gone English and had been shunned by her Amish friends and family, so he thought maybe she'd stay away.

It made his heart stir with strange feelings when he saw her wearing modern clothes. Her hair was cut short, and she was even wearing makeup. Such a contrast from the Anna Beachy he'd grown up and fallen in love with.

Silas glanced over at Rachel. Her shoulders drooped and tears rimmed her eyes; she looked exhausted. His heart twisted with the pain he saw on her face. If only she hadn't shut him out, he might be of some comfort to her now.

He shook his head slowly. Maybe it was best this way. She didn't trust him anymore, and he wasn't sure she should. After all, what had he ever done to make her believe he cared for her and not her sister? The truth was, until this very moment, he'd never seen Anna for what she really was—a modern woman who seemed much more comfortable in men's pants than she did in a long dress. She, who wanted his best friend—a drinking, loose-talking man, seeking out the fancy life and not caring who he hurt in the process.

Silas forced his attention to Bishop Weaver's words. "For as much as it has pleased the Almighty God to take unto Himself the soul of young Perry Beachy, we offer the body to this place prepared for it, that ashes may return to ashes. . .dust to dust. . .and the imperishable spirit may forever be with the Lord. Amen."

Rebekah Beachy sat slumped over in her wheelchair, audibly weeping. She clutched her husband's hand on one side, and her youngest daughter stood on her other side next to Joseph. The child was sobbing hysterically, and when her twin brother's coffin was lowered into the ground, Joseph lifted Elizabeth into his arms and carried her back to the buggy.

Silas felt strongly that he should speak to Rachel and Anna, too, for that matter. Now didn't seem the right time, though. There were too many others crowded around the grieving family, and he wanted the chance to speak with them in private.

I'll wait 'til later, he decided. *Maybe right after the funeral dinner.*

twenty

Since it was bitterly cold and there was snow on the ground, dinner had to be served inside the house. This meant everyone would be fed in shifts—the men first, then the women and children.

Rachel knew Anna would not be welcome to eat at any of the tables with her Amish friends and relatives, so she set a place for her in the kitchen at a small table near the fireplace. At first Anna argued, saying she wasn't hungry, but Rachel won out and Anna finally agreed to eat a little something.

When the meal was over, Rachel returned to the kitchen, hoping to speak to her sister before she returned home. When she saw Anna and their mother talking, she came to a halt just inside the kitchen door. Mom had tears in her eyes, and she was pleading with Anna to return home and reconcile herself with the church.

Anna shook her head and muttered, "I can't. My place is with Reuben now."

Rachel slipped quietly away, knowing Anna and Mom needed this time alone. She scurried up the steps and went straight to her room, realizing that she, too, needed a few minutes by herself. She'd been so busy helping with the funeral dinner and trying to put on a brave front in order to help others in the family who were grieving that she hadn't really taken the time to properly mourn.

Rachel stood in front of the window, staring out at the spiraling snowflakes. Her thoughts kept time with the snow—swirling, whirling, falling all around, then melting before she had the chance to sort things out.

"Why'd You have to take my little brother, God?" she murmured. "Why did Anna have to hurt our family by leavin' the faith?" She trembled involuntarily. "How come Silas has to pine away for Anna and can't see me as someone he could love?"

Deep in her heart Rachel knew none of these things were God's fault. He'd allowed them all right, but certainly He hadn't caused the bad things to happen. God loved Perry and had taken him home to heaven. Anna hadn't left home to be mean, either. She was obviously confused about her faith in God and was blinded by her love for Reuben. Love did strange things to people. Rachel knew that better than anyone. *Look how I wasted so many months hoping Silas would fall in love with me. It's not his fault he can't seem to get over his feelings for Anna. She hurt him real bad, and he might always hunger for his lost love.*

Rachel knew she would have to get on with her life. Maybe God wanted her to remain single. Might could be that her job was to run the greenhouse and take care of Mom and Dad. It was a bitter pill to swallow, but if it was God's will, she knew she must.

Rachel walked to the corner of her room. Maybe there was something in Anna's hope chest that she would like to have. Surely there were a few things she could put to good use in her new English home.

Rachel opened the lid and slowly began to remove each item. There were several hand towels, some quilted pot holders, and a few tablecloths—all things she was sure Anna could use. Next, she lifted out the beginning of a double-ring wedding quilt. Its colors of depth and warmth, in shades of blue and dark purple, seemed to frolic side-by-side.

Rachel's eyes filled with tears as she thought about her own hope chest, now empty and useless. She'd never even started a wedding quilt, and the few items she'd stored in the chest had either been sold or were on display at Thomas

Benner's store. Rachel had no reason to own a hope chest anymore, for she would probably never set up housekeeping with a husband and have *kinder.* Maybe God never planned for her to become a wife and mother.

Shoving her pain aside and reaching farther into the chest, Rachel discovered an old Bible and an embroidered sampler. Attached to the sampler was a note: *This was made by Miriam Stoltzfus Hilty. Given to my* mamm, *Anna Stoltzfus, to let her know that God has changed my heart.*

Rachel knew that Miriam Stoltzfus was Great-Aunt Mim and that Anna Stoltzfus was her great-grandma. She noticed there was also a verse embroidered on the sampler: *"A merry heart doeth good like a medicine," Proverbs 17:22.*

A sob caught in Rachel's throat as she read the words out loud. She clung to the sampler like it was some sort of life-line. The yellowing piece of cloth gave her a strange, yet comforting connection to the past.

Rachel's gaze came to rest on the old Bible. She laid the sampler aside and picked the Bible up, pulling open the inside cover. In small, perfectly penned letters were the following words: *"This* Biwel *belonged to Anna Stoltzfus. May all who read it find as much comfort, hope, and healing as I have found."*

Rachel noticed several crocheted bookmarks placed in various sections of the Bible. She turned the pages to some of the marked spots and read the underlined verses. One in particular seemed to jump right out. Psalm 71:14: "But I will hope continually, and will yet praise thee more and more." This was the very same verse Rachel had been reciting for the last several months. Was God trying to tell her something?

Rachel was about to turn the page when another underlined verse from Psalm 71 caught her attention. Verse 5 read: "For thou art my hope, O Lord God: thou art my trust from my youth."

Hot tears rolled down Rachel's cheeks as the words on the page burned into her mind. All this time Rachel had been hoping to win Silas's heart. She'd been praising God for something she hoped He would do. Never once had it occurred to her that the heavenly Father wanted her to put all her hopes in *Him.* She was to trust Him and only Him, and she should have been doing it since her youth. She'd been trying to do everything in her own strength because it was what *she* wanted. When Silas didn't respond as she'd hoped, Rachel's faith had been dashed away like sunshine on a rainy day.

Rachel broke down, burying her face in her hands. "Dear Lord, please forgive me. Help me learn to trust You more. Let my hope always be in You. May Your will be done in my life. Show me how best to serve You. Amen."

Rachel picked up the precious items she'd found in Anna's hope chest, slipped them into her apron pocket, and headed downstairs. The *Biwel* belonged to Anna's namesake and she should have it. The sampler belonged to Great-Grandma Anna's daughter, Miriam, and Anna should have that as well.

❧

Anna wasn't in the kitchen when Rachel returned. Mom was sitting at the table with her head bowed. Not wishing to disturb her mother's prayer, Rachel slipped quietly out the back door. She found Joseph and Pauline on the porch, sitting side-by-side on the top step. *They look so* gut *together,* Rachel mused. *I'm happy Joseph has found someone to love.*

Joseph turned around when Rachel closed the screen door. "Oh, it's you, little sister. Nearly everyone's gone home, and we didn't know where you were. Anna was lookin' for ya."

Rachel felt panic surge through her. "Did Anna leave?"

Joseph shook his head. "Naw, she said she wouldn't go without talkin' to you first."

"I think she took a walk down by the river," Pauline interjected. She removed her shawl and handed it to Rachel. "If you're goin' after her, you'd better put this on. It's mighty cold out today."

Gratefully, Rachel took the offered shawl. *"Danki.* I think I will mosey on down to the water and see if Anna's still there. I've got somethin' I wanna give her."

Rachel started out walking but soon broke into a run. The wind stung her face, but she didn't mind. Her only thought was on finding Anna.

☙

The rest of Silas's family had already gone home, but he wasn't ready to leave just yet. He wanted to hang around and see if he could offer comfort to Rachel. She hadn't looked right when he'd seen her earlier, and after lunch he'd gone looking for her, but she seemed to have disappeared. He figured she must be taking Perry's death pretty hard, and it pained him when she hadn't even responded to his hug. She felt small and fragile in his arms—like a broken toy he was unable to fix. It was as if Rachel was off in another world— in a daze or some kind of a dream world.

He remembered hearing his mom talk about her oldest sister and how she'd gone crazy when her little girl drowned in Paradise Lake. He didn't think Rachel would actually go batty, but she was acting mighty strange, and he couldn't go home until he knew she was going to be okay.

Silas decided to walk down to the river, knowing Rachel often went there to fish or look for birds. Just as he reached the edge of the cornfield, he spotted someone standing along the edge of the creek. His heart gave a lurch when he saw the figure leaning over the water. Surely, she wasn't thinking of—

Silas took off on a run. When he neared the clearing, he skidded to a halt. The figure he'd seen was a woman, but it wasn't Rachel Beachy. It was her sister. He approached Anna slowly, not wanting to spook her.

She turned to face him just as he stepped to the water's

edge. "Silas, you scared me. I thought I was all alone."

"Sorry. I sure didn't mean to frighten ya. I was lookin for—"

"I used to love comin' down here," she interrupted. "It was a good place to think. . .and to pray." Anna hung her head. "Sorry to say, I haven't done much prayin' since I left home. Guess maybe I should get back to it."

"Prayin' is *gut*," Silas agreed. "I think it goes hand in hand with thinkin'."

Anna smiled and pointed to the water. "Look, there's a big old catfish."

"Rachel likes to fish," Silas muttered.

Anna grinned. "I think you and my sister have a lot in common. She likes to spend hours feedin' and watchin' the birds that come into our yard, too."

Silas nodded. "I bought her a bird book and a pair of binoculars for her birthday."

"I'm sure she liked that."

"I thought so at the time, but now I'm not sure."

Anna touched the sleeve of Silas's jacket. "How come?"

He stared out across the water. "She thinks I don't like her. She thinks I'm still in love with you."

❧

Rachel stood behind the trunk of a white birch tree, holding her breath and listening to the conversation going on just a few feet away. She'd almost shown herself, but then she heard her own name mentioned, and she was afraid of what Anna and Silas were saying. Was Silas declaring his love for her sister? Was he begging her to leave Reuben and return to the Amish faith? Surely Silas must know the stand their church took against divorce.

"Who are you in love with, Silas?" she heard Anna ask.

Rachel pressed against the tree and waited breathlessly for his response. She was doing it again—eavesdropping. It wasn't right, but she could hardly show herself now, with Silas about to declare his love for Anna and all. Her thoughts went back to that day, many months ago, when Silas had said to Anna, "When you're ready, I'll be waitin'." Was he still waiting for her? Did he really think they had a chance to be together?

"I used to love you, Anna," she heard Silas say. "At least I thought I did." There was a long pause. "Guess maybe we'd been friends so long I never thought I'd fall in love with anyone but you."

"Have you, Silas?" Anna asked.

Rachel chanced a peek around the tree. Silas was standing so close to Anna he could have leaned down and kissed her. He didn't, though. Instead, he stood tall, shoulders back, and head erect. "You were right when you told me once that Rachel would be *gut* for me. I love her more'n anything, but I don't know what I can do to prove that love."

Feeling as if her heart could burst wide open, Rachel jumped out from behind the tree and leaped into Silas's arms, knocking them both over and just missing the water. "You don't have to do anything to prove your love!" she shouted. "What you said to Anna is proof enough for me!"

Silas looked kind of embarrassed as they scrambled to their feet, but Rachel didn't care. She turned to Anna with a wide smile. "I've got somethin' for ya."

"What is it?"

Rachel reached inside her apron pocket and withdrew the sampler and their great-grandma's Bible. "I found these at the bottom of your hope chest, and I think ya should have 'em."

Anna's eyes flooded with tears. "Great-Aunt Mim's Merry Heart sampler and Great-Grandma's *Biwel*. Mom gave them to me for my hope chest several years ago. I'd forgotten all about them."

Rachel handed the items over to her sister. "I read some passages in Great-Grandma Stoltzfus's *Biwel*. I found real hope in your hope chest, as I was reminded to put my hope in the Lord and keep trusting Him." She turned back to face Silas. "I thought I'd have to learn to live without your love, but now—"

Silas hushed her by placing two fingers against her lips. "Now you'll just have to learn to live as my wife." He leaned down to kiss her, and Rachel felt as if she were a bird—floating, soaring high above the clouds—reveling in God's glory and hoping in Him.

epilogue

Rachel stood on the lawn, her groom on one side, her brother Joseph and new sister-in-law Pauline on the other. It had been a *gut* wedding. Two double-ring wedding quilts were presented to the brides by their mothers, along with a double portion of happiness for both sets of newlyweds.

The only thing that could have made my day more complete would have been to share it with my older sister. On an impulse, Rachel glanced across the yard. To her amazement, Anna was walking toward her, holding a brown paper bag.

"Excuse me a minute," Rachel whispered to Silas. "There's someone I need to see."

Silas squeezed her hand. "Hurry back, *Frau.*"

Rachel smiled and slipped quietly away. She drew Anna off to one side, and they exchanged a hug. "It's so *gut* to see you. I was hopin' you'd receive my note about the weddin'."

"I didn't think I should come inside for the ceremony, under the circumstances and all. I did want to wish you well and give ya this." Anna handed the sack to Rachel.

"What is it?"

"Look inside."

Rachel opened the bag and reached in. Surprise flooded her soul as she withdrew a sampler. At first she thought it was the same one she'd given Anna last year, but when she read the embroidered words, she knew it wasn't. " 'For thou art my hope, O Lord God: thou art my trust from my youth,' Psalm 71:5."

"I thought it would be somethin' you could hand down to your children and grandchildren," Anna explained. She placed her hand against her stomach. "That's what I plan to do with the Merry Heart sampler Great-Aunt Mim made."

Rachel's eyes widened. "You're in a family way?"

Anna nodded and smiled. "The baby will come in the spring."

"Do Mom and Dad know they're gonna be grandparents?"

"I told them a few minutes before you came outside." Anna's eyes filled with tears. "They said they still love me, Rachel. They want me and Reuben to come visit after the baby is born." She glanced around the yard as though someone might be watching. "It's not really goin' against Bishop Weaver's ban for me to visit here or talk with my family now and then. Besides, Reuben and I had a long talk awhile back. We both want to stay English, but we've found a good church. We're readin' our Bibles again and prayin' together."

Rachel embraced her sister one more time. "I'm so happy to hear that, Anna, and I thank you for coming today." She held the sampler close to her heart. "I'll always cherish this, and every time I look at it, I'll not only be reminded to put my hope in Jesus, but I'll think of my English sister, who is also trustin' in God."

Anna smiled and ran her fingers through her short hair. "That's so true."

"Well, I'd best be gettin' back to my groom, or he'll likely come a-lookin' for me," Rachel said with a giggle.

Anna nodded. "Tell him I said to be happy and that he'd better treat my little sister right, or I'll come a-lookin' for *him*."

Rachel squeezed Anna's hand, then hurried toward Silas. She was so glad she'd opened her sister's hope chest last December, for if she hadn't, she might never have found the special sampler and the *Biwel* with God's Word, so full of hope.

When Rachel reached her groom, he pulled her to his side and whispered in her ear, *"Ich Leibe Dich*—I love you, and with you as my wife, I'll always be happy."

Rachel drew in a deep breath and leaned her head against his shoulder. "And I'll always love you."

A Letter To Our Readers

Dear Reader:

In order that we might better contribute to your reading enjoyment, we would appreciate your taking a few minutes to respond to the following questions. We welcome your comments and read each form and letter we receive. When completed, please return to the following:

Rebecca Germany, Fiction Editor
Heartsong Presents
PO Box 719
Uhrichsville, Ohio 44683

1. Did you enjoy reading *Ring of Hope* by Birdie L. Etchison?
   ❑ Very much! I would like to see more books
      by this author!
   ❑ Moderately. I would have enjoyed it more if

   _____

   _____

   _____

2. Are you a member of **Heartsong Presents**? Yes ❑ No ❑
   If no, where did you purchase this book?_____

   _____

3. How would you rate, on a scale from 1 (poor) to 5 (superior), the cover design?_____

4. On a scale from 1 (poor) to 10 (superior), please rate the following elements.

   _____ Heroine   _____ Plot

   _____ Hero   _____ Inspirational theme

   _____ Setting   _____ Secondary characters

5. These characters were special because_____
   _____
   _____

6. How has this book inspired your life?_____
   _____
   _____

7. What settings would you like to see covered in future
   Heartsong Presents books?_____
   _____
   _____

8. What are some inspirational themes you would like to see
   treated in future books?_____
   _____
   _____

9. Would you be interested in reading other **Heartsong
   Presents** titles?   Yes ☐   No ☐

10. Please check your age range:
    ☐ Under 18   ☐ 18-24   ☐ 25-34
    ☐ 35-45   ☐ 46-55   ☐ Over 55

Name _____

Occupation _____

Address _____

City _____ State _____ Zip _____

Email _____

Hearts♥ng

Any 12 Heartsong Presents titles for only $27.00*

CONTEMPORARY ROMANCE IS CHEAPER BY THE DOZEN!

Buy any assortment of twelve *Heartsong Presents* titles and save 25% off of the already discounted price of $2.95 each!

*plus $2.00 shipping and handling per order and sales tax where applicable.

HEARTSONG PRESENTS *TITLES AVAILABLE NOW:*

Hearts♥ng Presents
Love Stories
Are Rated G!

That's for godly, gratifying, and of course, great! If you love a thrilling love story but don't appreciate the sordidness of some popular paperback romances, **Heartsong Presents** is for you. In fact, **Heartsong Presents** is the *only inspirational romance book club* featuring love stories where Christian faith is the primary ingredient in a marriage relationship.

Sign up today to receive your first set of four never-before-published Christian romances. Send no money now; you will receive a bill with the first shipment. You may cancel at any time without obligation, and if you aren't completely satisfied with any selection, you may return the books for an immediate refund!

Imagine. . .four new romances every four weeks—two historical, two contemporary—with men and women like you who long to meet the one God has chosen as the love of their lives. . .all for the low price of $9.97 postpaid.

To join, simply complete the coupon below and mail to the address provided. **Heartsong Presents** romances are rated G for another reason: They'll arrive *Godspeed!*

www.heartsongpresents.com